TEN THOUSAND *CHARMS*

TEN THOUSAND CHARMS

WRITTEN BY LEANDER WATTS

Houghton Mifflin Company
Boston 2005

www.houghtonmifflinbooks.com

The text of this book is set in Centaur.

Library of Congress Cataloging-in-Publication Data
Watts, Leander.
Ten thousand charms / written by Leander Watts.
p. cm.
Summary: When an exiled German king and his three daughters arrive in Pharaoh,
New York, their fates become intertwined with that of an eleven-year-old ropemaker's apprentice
named Roddy whose supernatural abilities allow him to communicate with crows and dark forces.

ISBN 0-618-44897-7

[1. Supernatural—Fiction. 2. Crows—Fiction. 3. Kings, queens, rulers, etc.—Fiction.
4. Fathers and daughters—Fiction. 5. Immigrants—Fiction. 6. German Americans—Fiction.
7. Child labor—Fiction. 8. Human-animal relationships—Fiction.
9. New York (State)—History—1775-1865—Fiction.] I. Title.
PZ7.W339Te 2005
[Fic]—dc22

2004013184

ISBN-13: 978-0618-44897-5

Interior design and composition by Pamela Consolazio

Manufactured in the United States of America
WOZ 10 9 8 7 6 5 4 3 2 1

For Eileen

1

There was a king without a kingdom. There were three girls with no last names. And there was a boy without any parents.

The king's name was Ivars, actually Ivars the Seventh. He came from a tiny country in Germany that isn't there anymore. The land, yes. The woods and streams and even a few of the tottering, narrow, stone houses. Yes, those are still there. But the name is gone, the little kingdom of Schatzburg taken into a much bigger one, like a little pond swallowed up by a rising flood.

The girls were sisters, princesses in fact, daughters of the king. Kings don't need last names. There was only one King Ivars of Schatzburg. And so his girls didn't need last names either. They were just Wilhelmina, called Mina; Dorothea, called Thea; and Onyx, whom everyone knew as Nyxie.

Once, the boy had a father and mother, but they sold him to Mr. Queed to work as an apprentice in his great rope factory. He was ten when they sent him away. He was ten and a half when he was assigned to turn the great groaning crank. He was eleven when the Parliament of Crows took place.

2

That boy was called Roddy Whitelaw.

He was the lowest apprentice in the ropeworks, turning the crank, six days a week, on the rope-braiding machine. And there he was, listening to the creak of the wheels and the hum of the lines, the crunch of Mr. Queed's boots on the floor, the humphing of his breath as he struggled with the heavy ropes. There he was, like a strong little engine in the shape of a boy, making the rope strands twist and stretch and sing.

And he thought, It's like a great vast instrument. Strings tight as on a fiddle, making a low droning kind of song, the whole factory might have been built for sound, not to make endless spools of hemp rope.

These, of course, were not the kind of thoughts he was supposed to have at work. Indeed, he was not supposed to think at all. "When I want you to have an idea, I'll tell you what it is," Mr. Queed growled. "You just keep the crank

3

turning nice and steady and leave the thinking to your betters."

So Roddy was listening extra carefully to the hum of the ropes when he heard another, darker sound. A gathering of black wings. Hoarse shouts in the sky. Fluttering, beating, swirling, churning upward like a tempest with a mind of its own.

He wasn't the only one to hear it of course. Or see it. There was a single window in the whole of the ropeworks, and if he leaned away from the crank, he could see a corner of it. But Frank Beasling had gone to look out and he blocked Roddy's view.

Soon, others too had left their posts to see such a marvel. Roddy kept cranking. Mr. Queed kept on walking and gathering strands. But he shouted, "Get back to work! Go on. Get away from there."

Boys had left their places at the great hackling combs that prepared the hemp for braiding. They looked up through the window at the rushing whirlpool of black birds.

"Now!" Mr. Queed shouted. "Or you'll all, everyone of you, work till midnight tonight and all day Saturday."

This was a Friday, when the Parliament of Crows began.

Usually, if the apprentices were good, they'd get the afternoon off on Saturday. So they all went back to their hard work pretty fast.

But did they still hear the crows? Yes, indeed. Did they see them through the window? Yes, swirling swarms of blackness.

At first it sounded like shouts of anger, but then Roddy heard an almost friendly note, as though the only way crows have to greet one another is by screaming. Suddenly, they flew up in one huge swift squadron. Their shadow was splashed on the window. Then they, and their black uproaring voices, were gone.

3

King Ivars hadn't ever been interested in being a king. Of sitting on thrones and making decrees he had little interest. Of leading his tiny army or holding court he couldn't have cared less.

What Ivars really liked was to search out mysteries. Not crimes and cruelties, but strange things that no one could explain. The people of Schatzburg knew of his love of mysteries and they would come to the palace to show him what they'd found. A goat born with a patch of fur on his forehead in the shape of a perfect star. A toad that would only hop backward. A fossilized worm that looked just like the letter R. A baby boy who could already say his prayers in Latin.

King Ivars paid a few silver talers to anyone who might bring him such things. But his quest went further and deeper. For instance, he wanted to know about mummies in Egypt. And he read all he could about his great grandfather Ivars the Fourth who, rumor had it, could turn gold into lead (though not the other way around). He spent a whole week talking with an ancient, wrinkled gypsy lady who claimed she could read his mind. He wanted to know about the northern lights and the Southern Cross, the legend of King Frederick Iron Tooth and the tale of the two boys with three eyes.

Such things were what he most cared about. And so it was no surprise to anybody when soldiers came and told him he was no longer king of Schatzburg. The ruler of the neighboring land, Duke Karl Kristian Konrad, bought the loyalty of the Schatzburg servants and soon Ivars was a king with no kingdom.

Where to go? What to do? Ivars had been reading about America, especially a place just on the edge of the frontier, where it seemed all sorts of mysteries were happening. There, angels came down and spoke to farm boys. There, a deep, lonesome drum kept pounding in the night, but nobody could ever find it. Rattlesnakes still slithered and wolves still prowled in this place. And comets shone in the heavens too. Prophets rose up and said the end of the world was coming. People listened for Gabriel's trumpet, and some said they heard it.

"We're off to the New World," King Ivars told his three daughters. And so they began their long voyage west. They packed their trunks and loaded all the money they could gather into boxes bound with iron bands. And they went to the great seaport of Hamburg to catch a ship that would take them to America.

Some on the voyage talked of the wonderful farmland and glittering cities they'd find in America. Others were nervous, afraid of a new language, a new kind of government, red Indians, and strange foods. One boy on the ship could name all seven presidents, from George Washington to Andrew Jackson. He said the names over and over again, as though they were magic passwords that would get him into the new land.

But all Ivars cared about were the mysteries, or "charms" as he called them. By the time he landed in New York City, he knew ten words in English. Go, stop, hot, cold, ship, captain, king, girl, look, and charm.

That's what he called the strange events, the mysterious objects, the meteorites and two-headed cats, the rivers that flowed backward and the stone giants that the Indians claimed used to roam the land.

"Ten thousand charms," Ivars would say, writing in his big, leather-bound book. "We're going to the land of ten thousand charms."

4

"Did you ever see such a thing?"

"It means summer will come soon."

The boys were all gathered behind the ropeworks, after they'd had their supper. "All" sounds like a lot. In fact there were only five of them.

"No, you dunce. It means that spring will last twice as long."

"None of that," Frank Beasling said, cuffing Charlie Near on the head. "It's got nothing to do with the weather or the seasons. It's an omen. You know what that means?

"It's an omen of ill tidings, that's what it is," Frank declared. He was the type of boy who always thought he knew more than he really did. Big words, big ideas, and bossing around when he could. "Ill omens, war, and rumors of war."

"Oh shut it, you great lump of dung," Lester Fingal said. "It was just a bunch of birds." He always managed to have a little tobacco for chewing. That evening wasn't any different. He spat a wad of brown juice within an inch of Frank's shoe and Roddy thought they'd get to fighting right fast.

Usually that meant he needed to get out of there. They were both bigger than him, Lester was meaner, and Frank could always manage to get the blame pinned on somebody else.

Still, Roddy stayed, watching the others puff up their chests and throw curses back and forth. He backed off some, to get out of their way quickly, if he had to. But he stayed till it was clear no fight would happen. Lester spat another gob of ambeer. Frank used some words nobody else knew. But neither of the boys set to shoving, which was usually how fights got going. With the first shove came the first punch. And then there was no turning back.

This time the fight sputtered out and the two of them separated. Frank went off to sulk and mutter threats. Lester got out his dice and rattled them in his hand. "Anybody game?"

Charlie Near nodded and the two of them went off to the barn where Mr. Queed wouldn't see them gambling.

That left Roddy standing there with Uriah Nottworth. Of all the apprentices, Uriah was the slowest to learn, and the fastest to forget. He was clumsy and didn't talk very clearly and of course the others all made fun of his name. "Not worth the scrapings he's made out of," Frank announced every time Uriah made a mistake. "Not worth a paper penny."

"Over to the old Seven place," Uriah said now, slow and unsure. "I went over there." Years back, a family called Severin had lived on that farm, and ever since, people thereabouts had cut the name down to Seven. "There's girls there."

"What are you talking about?" As long as Roddy had been apprentice at the ropeworks, the Seven house had been empty. Something about a curse, or bad omens, kept anyone from buying it.

"I seen them when I went down to Malcolm's for the milk," Uriah said. "Three girls. Real pretty. They was out doing wash in the tub and hanging it up. Pretty dresses, all sorts of colors. Never seen such a thing. Just yesterday. Or maybe the day before. I seen them but they didn't look over to me. Talking real funny."

Roddy was the only one Uriah ever confided in. The others were too cruel, or couldn't be bothered trying to figure out what he was saying. "You're not just making this up?"

"No, sir, indeed," Uriah said. "Three girls pretty as finches.

I watched them hang up the wash. All sorts of colors. Green and pink and blue just like the sky."

Roddy had an hour before dark. So he went down the road to the old Seven place to see what he could see.

The whole way there, crows were flocking above him, huge swirling clouds of them. It scared him. To be all alone, walking the road, with sunset looming and the dark shouting tempest clouds above his head. "Black angels," Roddy said to himself. Then out loud, "An army of black angels." This didn't make it any less strange, but it calmed him a little to put a name on something he'd never seen before today. Suddenly, as though they'd heard him, the crows flew off. They moved in dark fluttering squadrons, shrieking, laughing, crying, yelling, and perhaps even preaching in some lost language.

5

King Ivars stood in the doorway of his ramshackle house, watching the birds swoop and soar. He had a heavy book bound in sharkskin and a goose quill pen to write down what he saw. But he just stood there, staring.

"Papa, come in before you catch your death of cold." Even in this harsh new land, Mina was ever a princess. She gave orders as though she still had a half dozen noble ladies and three beautiful carriages waiting for her.

Now she tugged on her father's sleeve. But he paid her no mind. The crows were amazing, like fragments of the night sky torn and fluttering in daylight.

"Papa, do as you're told," Mina said. All three of the girls spoke German to their father. They'd had an English governess back in Schatzburg, and could speak their new tongue fairly well. But King Ivars still, after only a month in America, needed them to translate everything when he dealt with the people in his new home.

"The Parliament of Crows," Ivars said. "I read years ago of this thing. But to see it, to hear it, is a wonder and an astonishing charm. I was right, daughter, to bring us here. This is our first charm here in this beautiful valley."

He called it beautiful because it was. Broad and green and serene. But he also knew that the name of the river, Genesee, was an Indian word that meant "beautiful valley." English words, Iroquois names, his German, and all the Latin of his scholarly books: for Ivars language was a soup made of a dozen different ingredients. And his mind was the cauldron, where all the words boiled and mingled and churned.

"Something uncanny this way comes," Ivars said, as his second daughter, Thea, joined him to watch. "It's a sign. Surely a sign from heaven. Once every fifty years the crows gather in their parliament to talk and argue and sometimes to decide."

Like him, she'd never seen such a thing. But in her was fear, not fascination. Since leaving the old country, everything seemed a threat to Thea. She glimpsed danger where her father saw only delight.

"You know you'll catch a cold," Mina scolded. It wasn't illness that troubled Thea though. Rather, she was afraid of something new and strange.

Mina gave up on her father and went back to her sewing. The youngest of the three girls, Nyxie, now started complaining that the wind was blowing dirt into the house. Her voice was high and quavery, full of whining anger. "Papa, shut that door!"

Thea stayed with him, watching the swirls of black birds.

Now the sun was nearing the horizon. It seemed to go down slower here. In Germany, there was less warning, less of a slide from light to dark. Her father explained they were farther south here in York State in America, and so sunsets were different than in the old country.

But Thea was convinced something that simple couldn't explain the slower sunsets. Everything was different now. The strange animals, the crude foods, the language, the clothes, the money, and even the skies.

She huddled close to her father as another gust of wind pummeled them.

"There," Ivars said. "On the road." He pointed to a boy coming toward them, walking fast with a long staff to help him along. "Who is that boy?" Thea had never seen him before. Small and thin, with shaggy hair and a tattered coat, he looked like a vagabond who'd been on the road for days.

6

It had only taken Roddy Whitelaw an hour to walk from town out to the Seven place. He'd set off because of the three beautiful girls that Uriah had told him about. However, seeing the crows again, his thoughts were only on the skies.

He watched the patterns that the crows made. And it seemed they were writing messages on the blue vault of heaven. A thousand black smudges of ink, the crows scribbled on the sky. Letters? Words? Pictures? The markings came and went so fast, Roddy could make no sense of them.

Standing on the crest of the hill, leaning on his walking staff, he peered upward.

Only when Roddy heard the door slam down below at the old Seven house did he remember why he'd come. And already the sun was near setting. His idea had been just to watch from a distance, maybe hide and get a little glimpse of the girls.

That plan was gone now. An old man was staring straight

at him. And one of the girls too. She had dark hair, twisted up and pinned on her head. Her dress was no beautiful gown, as Uriah had said, but simple homespun. Still, Uriah had not imagined things. This girl was pretty indeed. She was different, though, from the ones Roddy saw in church or walking slowly to school, who were hoping to be noticed. She was afraid. Roddy could see that even from a distance. Still, she did not flee inside and slam the door.

Of a sudden, the crows went silent. They were in the trees now, perhaps roosting for the night. The cawing ceased and a strange peace fell on the farmstead.

Roddy felt a bit of a fool, standing there. Surely the other boys would learn that he'd come to see the girls, and he'd be teased to torment for it.

The old man said something to his daughter, and she nodded. "Boy!" she shouted. "You, boy! Come down here."

He was about to head back to town, but she called again, not so harshly this time. "Have you ever seen such a thing? My father wants to know if this happens here all the time." The sound of her voice stirred the crows. Roddy saw them rustling in the treetops. But they calmed and didn't take flight again.

"Can you answer him some questions?"

Roddy shrugged and went down the pathway to the house. The old man was wearing clothes such as Roddy had never seen. The coat was huge with a hundred folds, rich purple cloth pocked with little silvery buttons. His boots, too, were loose, made of soft doeskin, not the stiff cowhides that Roddy's shoes were fashioned from. The old man had a beard, bushy and wild and mostly white.

He spoke to the girl in a strange tongue, and the girl translated. "My father wants to know if you have lived here long, and if you have seen such a thing before."

Roddy shook his head. "Yes, no, I mean I've never seen this before and I'm from around here, over to Rector's Ford. I'm one of Mr. Queed's boys." He said too much, too fast. And she didn't understand it all. "At the ropeworks. I didn't live here before but now I work for him, so I left my home."

"Is this Rector's Ford a place? A city near here? Is that correct?"

The girl had a charming accent, at least to Roddy's ears, turning "this" into "ziss" and "that" into "zatt," and almost purring when she said words full of r's. Sometimes she stopped in the middle of speaking, trying to find the right way to say something in English.

"Just a little village, a half dozen houses and a tavern. Don't even have a church."

"So this is truly strange, the black birds? How do you call them?"

"Crows. And it surely is. I never seen so many in my whole entire life."

She explained to her father what Roddy had said, then asked, "You know of other charms? My father has brought us here because he heard this place is rich with them."

"What do you mean, 'charms'?"

She struggled for the right words. "The once-in-a-century happening, the freak of nature, miracles and astonishing signs."

"I'm just a rope-monkey, that's all. I don't know about such things."

The door opened and the other two girls peered out. "Who is it, Thea? What does he want?"

"Just a boy from town. Papa wanted to talk with him."

The old man rifled through his book and pointed to a complicated drawing. Roddy couldn't understand a bit of it. It seemed to be a sky chart, showing the moon and the sun and various stars. But some had faces, and one wore a crown.

Roddy knew about constellations, the Great Bear and the Swan and the Serpent. But he didn't recognize any of these figures.

"I should be going now," he said. "If I'm not back for evening prayers, I'll get a whipping for sure."

The old man took his hand and shook it. It was warm and strong, much stronger than Roddy expected. "You come back again," the old man said.

Thea translated, making sure Roddy understood. But she gave him no smile nor parting hand. Just a cold, steady gaze.

7

When they were forced to flee Schatzburg, Ivars brought more than money — he brought his books. Duke Karl Kristian Konrad had no fear that Ivars might return with an army to fight for the throne. Ivars cared so little for ruling and reigning that it took him three days to realize that he was no longer king of Schatzburg. So a trunk of silver talers and a wagonload of books were enough to make sure King Ivars would never return.

Now in America, in the western reaches of York State, in the valley of the Genesee, Ivars lived much as he had in the old country. No servants, no castle or crown, but he had his books and his girls and that was all that mattered to him.

So the first day of the Crows' Parliament, he stared up at the black legions in the sky, then he paged through book after book, trying to find some explanation. "Unheimlich, unheimlich," he kept saying to his daughters. "Wunderbar unheimlich." This meant "wonderfully strange" and was for Ivars the best that something could be.

He was happy, truly happy, for the first time since leaving the old country. With just rumors and scraps of news, he'd made the right choice and come to the right place.

The girls were not so sure. Winters would be fierce here. And though most of the Iroquois had been pushed west or into Canada, still the girls heard stories of terrible bloody crimes committed by renegade Indians. The food certainly was not as good in America, as Nyxie was apt to say at every meal. And there were no fine shops where they could buy new dresses. This was the worst thing for Mina, living, as she said, "like a peasant." No orchestra to play for balls and dancing. No ladies in waiting. No handsome soldiers jingling by on beautiful horses.

And no church bells. That was what Thea missed most. In the old country, she could hear every hour of the day, somber, dark bells tolling. And even in the black of night, sometimes she'd lay awake in her great canopied bed and listen to the bells in St. Gottfried's tower.

The girls had to work now too. In Schatzburg they had had dozens of servants. Here, they had to do all the household tasks. And though they complained about the harsh lye soap and the blisters they got from splitting stove wood, Thea didn't really mind. In fact, she took a little joy from being useful, and not just a pretty ornament that could do nothing worthwhile.

That night, when the sun slid away into dark oblivion, they huddled close to the fire. Mina was in charge of keeping it going. She would allow neither of her sisters to place a single stick into the flames. Oldest, but not wisest, of the girls, Mina insisted that the others obey her as though she were their mother.

"I am not going to tell you again, Nyxie. You're not a baby anymore. Keep your hands away from there!"

King Ivars paid no attention to their bickering. He sat with a book tilted so that the pages were painted crimson by the fire. He muttered and nodded and ran his finger under the words, like a little boy just learning to read.

"Papa, you need to get your rest," Thea said, hoping her father would listen. "You're going to hurt your eyes reading in this terrible light." In Schatzburg they had great candelabra with a hundred bright flames on each. Here, it was only dim fire glow, or a few sputtering tallow rushlights.

Back at home, Thea thought, we had a whole castle. And here we have a few dark dingy rooms. "Papa, it's time for you to rest your eyes."

Mina was doing her tatting, as ladies often did in the old country. But where could she use such a beautiful little patch of lace? They needed blankets for winter, not delicate decorations for a gown. Still, Mina would not give up the hope that someday they'd return to Schatzburg. And so she tried, even in this crude little house, to still be a princess.

Thea had given up hope. That world was lost forever.

"Papa, are you paying attention?" He nodded but kept reading with his nose practically touching the page. "It's hopeless," she sighed. "You're all hopeless."

She got up and put on her shawl.

"Where do you think you're going at this hour?" Mina snapped.

"I don't think. I know. Out." Thea slammed the door behind herself.

The old Seven house looked even more feeble in the dark. A little firelight shone in one window. But silhouetted against the swaying hemlocks, the house might have been a play toy cut out of black paper. The roof was pointier than on other farmhouses. And the windows narrower. Thea looked back at her new home and now it seemed the house itself was swaying in the wind.

She thought of the crows, hidden and silent. In the trees all around, she knew, they were roosting, waiting for dawn to explode again into noise and flight.

Walking down the trail to the well, she heard something low and whispery. Though it was more a snake's hiss than a human voice, she was sure she heard words in it: "pretty, pretty, pretty."

Her heart clenched in her chest. She felt a cold tendril of wind curl around her feet. The darkness seemed to grow darker.

Thea was brave, but she was not foolish. As fast as she could move, she was back in the house. Her father looked up. "It's nothing," she said. "I just got a little scared." She didn't want her father to know, to go out there in the cold with a torch, searching around. It was probably just a skunk or a raccoon, she told herself. "Nothing. Nothing at all." She forced her breathing to calm. She sat by the fire and kept telling herself that no voice had whispered, "pretty, pretty, pretty" from the shadows.

Mina shook her head, as though Thea were feeble-minded.

Her father went back to his book, and Thea went to the window. She looked out a long time, but saw only dark trees and a star-pocked sky.

8

Roddy Whitelaw was looking out another window at the same stars. He'd escaped the house where he lived with the other boys, and crouched in the dark, in the rope factory. With the pulleys silent, the great lines all limp and still, the cranks no longer moving round and round, the ropeworks stretched out like a vast tomb.

Mr. Queed was proud of his factory, always boasting to anyone who'd listen. "One thousand feet long! Pace it off yourself. Go on, measure it. One thousand feet. Three hundred and thirty yards. Sixty-six rods. However you measure it, I've got the biggest ropewalk in all of York State."

Now quiet and motionless, the great narrow building seemed to extend on forever into shadow.

Usually the boys avoided the ropewalk after work. They were there ten hours a day. Why go back when they were free? But Roddy had discovered the huge, beautiful silence. And he'd go off sometimes after supper, if he thought none of the others would notice.

He stared through the grimy window like a prisoner looking through his iron bars. Six more years. Six years of winding the crank and untangling the lines. Six years of listening to Mr. Queed shout orders and curses. It seemed forever to Roddy. By then he'd almost be a man, free to do as he pleased.

Would he go back to Rector's Ford to see his parents? Would they even want him back? He hated them for sending him off as an apprentice. But they were his mother and father, and so how could he hate them? He wanted to be back there. He wanted, quite simply, to be wanted. But they had eight other children. He was just a name they barely remembered and a mouth they could barely feed.

"Hey!" The voice jolted him like a crack of lightning.

He turned from the window, peering into the looming darkness of the ropewalk.

"What are you doing here?" It was Frank Beasling.

"Nothing," Roddy said. But he knew that wouldn't satisfy Frank.

"That's a lie. You're such a liar," Frank said. "I saw you go out after prayers. The others are playing cribbage. Playing cards is evil. Gambling is evil. They know that and they do it anyway. I should tell on them. Mr. Queed would give them all six hours extra if he knew."

Frank came closer. Draped in shadow, he looked even more like a great hairless weasel. His eyes were too small for his face. His lips puckered and pursed when he wasn't talking. "So what are you doing here?"

"I told you, nothing."

"And I told you, you're a dirty liar."

He knew Roddy wouldn't fight. He could heap all the insults he wanted on Roddy, and not risk a bloody nose. "I asked you a question."

"Who died and left you in charge?" Roddy said.

"Keep that up and I'll tell Mr. Queed. I got my eye on you, Whitelaw. I'm watching every move you make."

And with that he slunk back into the shadows. Roddy could never understand how somebody so clumsy at work could move so silently. He was gone in a few heartbeats. And the silence returned, like blackness rushing in after a door is closed.

9

King Ivars had chosen western York State because of all the strange happenings he'd read about. But it was a big place, two hundred miles from end to end. Where to settle?

As they rode the waves heading across the ocean toward the New World, Ivars pored over maps. And one day, with the sun burning bright and hot at high noon, he looked down at his map and saw the name "Pharaoh."

"There," he said, pointing to the town and pulling Thea to come look. "Right there. Pharaoh, York State. That must be the place for us."

It was near the river he'd read about, the Genesee. "Due north," Ivars said to Thea, tracing the wiggling line upward on his map. "Straight north, like the Nile. The whole way, due north."

And so it was decided. They landed at Castle Garden on the tip of Manhattan. And within two days, they were headed north on a Hudson River schooner and then east on an Erie Canal packet boat. And after a long, jolting, rumbling stage-coach ride, they came to Pharaoh.

From such a name, Thea had expected pyramids and camels. Instead she found shacks and shanties, a little white church, and pigs in the street. "My papa wants to buy a house," Mina explained when they'd arrived at the only inn in Pharaoh. But Thea's English was better, and Ivars told her to translate.

"We've come a long way. We have good money. We can pay. Is there a house here for us?"

The innkeeper was no help. But there was a lawyerman, small and oily and constantly rubbing his fingers together, who took them out to the old Seven house and said they could have it for a song.

"A song?" Mina said. "What do you mean?"

"It's an expression," Thea explained. "He means it will be cheap. Not so dear."

"Yes, yes," the lawyerman said. "Not nearly so dear as some other places."

So Ivars unpacked the money trunk and paid the lawyerman in silver talers, and they had their home in the New World.

10

Roddy worked hard at the great crank. Round and round while Mr. Queed moved up and down the ropewalk, braiding the endless lengths of hemp.

Some of the other boys were at the hackling combs, hitting and dragging the hemp fibers through the iron teeth. Frank Beasling, as the senior apprentice, watched over them to make sure they didn't slack off or slow down. Over the drone of the wheel and the singing of the tight marlines, Frank liked to tell terrible stories of boys who didn't do their job properly. Charlie and Lester paid him no mind, but Uriah listened closely and it made him even clumsier to think of the awful fate that waited for careless boys.

"Had one here two years back," Frank hissed, leaning near to Uriah. "Got his hand cut off by the ace-line. Got sloppy and the line sliced it clean off. You want to watch yourself or you'll end up in five pieces. And we'll throw you to the dogs."

He poked Uriah in the chest, almost snarling now at him.

"You're going to be next if you don't watch what you're doing."

Roddy had had enough, too much, of Frank's needling.

"Leave him alone," Roddy said. But the whining of the wheel drowned out his voice.

"What did you say?" Frank came over and jabbed Roddy with his sharp, bony finger.

"I said, leave Uriah alone. He's clumsy enough without you pestering him all the time."

Arguing with Frank made Roddy lose the rhythm of the crank. Mr. Queed looked down the long ropewalk, like a spider sighting along his sticky line of web. "What's going on there?" he shouted.

Frank said, "This boy is not minding his —"

"Get back to work," Mr. Queed shouted. "Both of you. We've got orders for three thousand feet and nobody's leaving here until it's all done and packed in the wagons."

Frank gave Roddy an evil look, and a worse whispered curse. Then he said louder, "You're in trouble, boy, dire serious trouble," and went back to work.

The rest of the afternoon, the rope factory seemed like a nightmare that Roddy could not wake from. The pulleys and booms squealed like sick animals. Lines creaked and moaned.

Everything seemed a danger, like a weird labyrinth that had trapped him and would hold him forever.

Mr. Queed came toward Roddy, braiding his way along the lines. He was an ugly man, with tufts of hair that stuck out from the sides of his head, and a nose like a swollen wart. That day, that afternoon, he seemed ten times worse, glaring at Roddy as he came nearer and nearer.

Ten feet away, five feet, standing close enough to touch him — Mr. Queed loomed up big and awful. His eyebrows stood out like the feelers on a beetle. His lips were pulled back, showing his yellowy teeth.

"Keep it steady, boy." That's all he said. "Keep it steady."

Then he turned and headed back, having completed a length and starting a new one.

Roddy's arm went round and round, twisting the lines. And it seemed this would be his fate forever.

11

The boys worked late, till the wagons were loaded and ready to go off early the next morning.

They ate their supper in the great room of Mr. Queed's house, all around one trestle table. An old woman named Mother Fecula was the cook and housekeeper there. While the boys ate, Fecula stood in the shadows, quiet as sleep. She was shaped like an old turnip. And the straggly hairs on her face made her look even more like an ancient root.

The boys said their evening prayer and then set to eating.

Like most nights, it was a watery potato soup with a few shreds of grayish meat floating on top. Roddy thought it might be mutton. But Lester and Charlie whispered that the little flecks of gristly meat were all that remained of Mr. Queed's least favorite apprentices. Still, Roddy had worked hard since sunup, and his dinner had only been a biscuit and lukewarm coffee. So he wolfed down as much as he could, before Mr. Queed stood and rapped a serving spoon on the table.

"I have evidence," he began, "strong evidence, that certain of you boys have been taking part in gambling games. You know that I will not tolerate such behavior. Dice are the Devil's bones. The rattle of dice is the rattle of death. And playing cards are the Devil's looking glass. You hold a card in your palm and you see yourself, tricked out in fancy clothes, a king or a prince or a knight. But it's all falsehood!" His voice was rising, like a storm heading for them.

"You will suffer more than you can imagine, if you play at cards! Suffer here, in this world. Shame and loss and debt. And suffer in the next world too. For the gates of heaven are closed forever against a gambler!"

He was silent for a long while. And this was worse than the shouting. He stared each boy in the eye, searching him for some sign of guilt.

"Uriah Nottworth. Stand!" Mr. Queed growled.

"I didn't do it. Honest and truly, I never touched no dice nor cards." Uriah was shaking, already close to tears. "Never once. I'm a good boy. Truly I am."

"See that you stay that way. Mind me! I have my eye on you.

And when I'm not watching, then Mother Fecula is." The old woman shuffled out of the shadows, pointed with a knotty finger at Uriah, and then disappeared back where she'd come from.

"Yes, sir. I surely will." He stood there trembling.

"You think you can hide your guilt, but I can see the mark of the Devil's bones there in your hands. Just once. You touch dice just once, and you're marked forever." He nodded and Uriah collapsed into his seat.

"Some of you think you're clever and can fool me. But I tell you, just once I catch you with dice or cards and you will regret it forever."

He pushed back his plate, where a nice juicy beefsteak had lain. "Now go to your room. And meditate on my words."

The boys all rose and filed out, murmuring "good night" as they passed by Mr. Queed.

12

Frank Beasling, as the senior boy, was allowed to carry the candle. He led the others in single file to the one long room attached to the back of the house. When the door was closed, the boys relaxed some. Lester snorted and shook his head. "That old fool. If dice is all we got to worry about then we're doing pretty fine, I'd say. Seems to me being hungry is a lot worse than some little blot on my soul."

"You watch what you say," Frank snarled at him. "I'll tell him every word."

"And I'll break your legs in three places," Lester said, smiling at him, stretching out in his bed.

"You think you're so clever," Frank said. "But you'll pay. One of these days you'll pay a fearsome price."

"There's the stinkpot." Lester pointed to the bucket they used when it was too cold to go to the outhouse. "Go stick your head in it."

Frank puffed and sneered, but the argument dwindled down to nothing. They all were exhausted. And they'd be up again, and at work, mighty soon.

Roddy lay on his bed, sliding fast into sleep. He thought about his mother and father, as he did almost every night. Why did he have to be here, with these boys? Why couldn't he go home? Seven years of hard work and bad food and a cold bed and trying every day to keep from being whipped.

Frank blew out the candle and the darkness poured into every crack and cranny of the room.

Charlie Near slept next to Roddy. And he always spent a long time rolling and wriggling, making the cords of the bed creak. Roddy counted. Back and forth, back and forth.

"You done all right," Charlie whispered.

"What?" Roddy roused a little. "You say something?"

"You done the right thing, telling Frank to leave Uriah alone. He's a dunce, but he didn't do nobody no harm. Someone ought to punch Frank's teeth down his throat."

Lester must have heard this, adding, "And kick him in the guts."

Now Roddy was awake. He pulled his blanket around his shoulders and sat up. Frank was already snoring, like a set of bellows heaving in and out. "How come Mr. Queed lets him boss us around?"

"Because Frank is a tattletale and a spy. Maybe he's listening right now." Charlie got up and looked at Frank. A little moonlight spilled into the room, thin and watery. "No. He's out good and solid. Must be all that hard work telling us what to do."

Lester whispered, "That time we went into town to the singing school, Frank tagged along so we wouldn't do nothing bad. He knew we went just to see the girls. I can't sing two notes. And Charlie's got a voice like a bullfrog. But you should've seen the girls there. I'm telling you, pretty and all decked out. And when they sang their part, it was a rain of silver coming right out of heaven."

Charlie got back into bed. "Uriah said there was three girls living at the old Seven place. Pretty like he never seen in his whole life."

"Since when does Uriah know anything about girls? It was probably a couple of stray pigs." They both laughed, though not very loud.

"No, it's true," Roddy said. "I saw them too. Three girls and an old man with a big white beard. They don't talk American.

Well, the old man doesn't. And the girls, you can tell, they came from the old country."

"We ought to sneak over some night and see what we can see."

"The old Seven place? At night? Include me out," Charlie said. "There's something serious bad living there. I'll bet you those girls won't last a week at that place."

"They already been there a month," Lester said.

"I still say I'm keeping good and far from there."

"You're talking like an old lady. There ain't no such thing —"

"There's something, I tell you, something fearsome bad."

Roddy was falling asleep. He wanted to listen, to ask them questions. But he couldn't keep his mind up above the surface anymore. Sleep came on, sure as the tide. Charlie and Lester were still talking, about something they called "the black ghast," about weird noises in the dark and the flash of yellowy eyes, as Roddy slid into the dark nothing.

13

The Parliament of Crows continued the next day. And King Ivars went out with his writing book and great quill pen to take notes. The birds were massing a little farther away from town, like clouds of black smoke from some terrible fire.

"Unheimlich," Ivars kept muttering, as he hiked over hill and gully. "Wunderbar unheimlich." Seeing that he was going farther afield that day, Thea went along so there'd be no trouble. He was heading away from Pharaoh. But if the crows turned and went toward town, then her father might end up in another argument.

Usually, when he shouted in German and tried to make the townsfolk understand, Thea stood by, saying everything over in English. She was the best at translating. But more important, she was the most patient with the little king's moods and shrill storming.

"Ach! Ach!" he'd shouted at the blacksmith the week before.

"Du kackenkopf." Thea had smiled uncomfortably and said, "What he means to say is the circle needs to be bigger." The little king had paid the blacksmith to make some special astronomical instrument. And the blacksmith hadn't understood the plans very well. She had had to lead the king away before he got into a real fight.

They were standing together under an old copper beech tree, staring up into the branches, when they saw Roddy again, coming down the lane.

The crows had been chattering and shouting for hours. But as Roddy approached, a quiet fell. And as he reached the great tree, the silence was complete.

Ivars stared at him in wonder. "They wait on his word," the king said, looking over the shabby, dirty boy. "They know him." And though Thea had heard her father spout a hundred nonsensical explanations, this time she wondered if he was right. The crows weren't just silent. They seemed to be expecting something. How many hundred thousands of bright berry black eyes were now peering down at them from the trees?

"What does it mean?" Ivars said in German. "Ask him what it means."

those times. Shaking and woozy and not all there. But this wasn't drunkenness. It was something much deeper, more true.

"My father thinks the crows have gathered to make a decision," Thea told him. "Is it true that they have come from all around to decide?"

"That's right," Roddy said slowly. "They decided. And they have a new king." He had no idea what this meant. The words just came out of him, like honey flowing from sun-warmed combs.

The old man came close and put his hands on Roddy's shoulders. "You look," he said in English. "Look."

Roddy peered up into Ivars's eyes. They were pale as thaw water, a weak liquid blue. But they still saw clearly. Roddy knew that. The old man looked at him, and into him, and then said something that Thea had to translate.

"He says we are a very long way from home. And we will never go back. This is our new home, and it is the right place. He knows that now. We came to see the Ten Thousand Charms. Or do you say 'wonders'? Is that the right word?"

King Ivars rattled on some more in German, still holding on to Roddy.

"He says you are not like the others here. You can see what

they cannot. You can hear, while when they listen, there is only silence."

Roddy had come out that day just to get another peek at the girls. Mr. Queed and Charlie and Uriah had taken the wagons to deliver all the rope they'd made. Frank was left in charge, but he was busy spying on Lester, so Roddy thought he had a few hours free.

He just wanted to see the girls. He had no thoughts about crows or strange old men or wondrous happenings when he set out. After so many days imprisoned at the ropeworks, he just wanted to see something pretty.

Now Ivars held him close and stared like a fiery-tongued preacher into his eyes.

"See! See!" Ivars said, letting go and opening a canvas sack. "You see."

Roddy looked carefully inside but it seemed to contain only darkness. Ivars stuck his hand in and pulled out a snake's skeleton.

Roddy jerked away backward. Even though not a shred of flesh remained on the white bones, it still had fangs, and the rattle made its dry hissing sound. Thea said, "We have none of these in the old country. You call them rattlesnakes?"

Ivars shook the skeleton, and it seemed to come to life, writhing and rattling.

Roddy could neither run nor come close for a better look, though he wanted to do both. Ivars looked like a wild man, his white beard billowing around his face and the snake seeming to wriggle though it was long dead.

"You've seen these around here?" Thea asked.

They were rare now in York State, like the wolves and bears and badgers and foxes. But yes, he had seen one once.

Perhaps it was his earliest memory. A little boy playing on the rocky slope behind their farmhouse. A buzzing noise that seemed both beautiful and terrifying. Then the snake was there staring little Roddy in the eyes. He was barely old enough to talk then. He didn't know about rattlesnakes. And so he reached out to touch it. The snake reared back, ready to strike with those glittering fangs.

Roddy had said his name, like a baby wizard casting his first spell. Just one word: "Roddy." And the snake didn't strike. It slunk away as though it knew he was no threat.

So now with Ivars shaking the skeleton at him, he might have been back ten years before.

The king put the snake away, and took a deep breath. He

stared at Roddy, as though trying to see something in a swirling mist. He spoke quietly. Thea's voice wasn't much louder. "You have no mother or father?"

"I work for Mr. Queed."

"But what about your parents? Where are they?"

"Back at home. There are nine of us, so they needed to send me out to be an apprentice." He tried to sound easy and unconcerned about it, as when the subject came up with the other boys. "I don't care," he said. But Thea, and even Ivars, who didn't understand the words, knew this wasn't true. "It doesn't matter one way or the other," Roddy continued.

"You never see them?" Thea asked.

"Not since I came here." Roddy didn't want to talk about it. Not then, not ever. It was bad enough feeling all confused and turned around. But if Thea asked any more questions, he was afraid he'd start crying.

Roddy said, "What about you? Where's your mother?"

"She is gone," Thea said. "Back to heaven. That is how Papa says it. Gone back to be with the angels."

Ivars dug in one of his big baggy pockets and pulled out a little chunk of blue-black stone. He jabbered away in German, and Thea struggled to keep up.

"He says it fell from the sky. A shower of hot sparks. Falling stars. What do you call them here? *Meteorstein?* Do you know that word in English? It is metal, he says. Not stone. He says it is iron from the sky, and it has powers, but he has not learned how to unleash the powers yet. Shooting stars. Is that how you say it?"

Ivars grabbed Roddy by the hand and gave him the little nub of metal. With the first touch, Roddy felt weak and strange. Ivars pressed it hard into his palm, and Roddy thought he might pass out. He tottered, like the people in church when the holy power came down.

The old man helped him sit down on the ground. He crouched there beside Roddy, like a doctor making sure he was not in danger.

Roddy was woozy, and very tired all of a sudden.

Ivars asked a question, and Thea translated. "Why do you work for Mr. Queed?"

"We signed papers," Roddy whispered. "I have a contract. My father signed me away for seven years."

"And he got money for you? Mr. Queed pays him?"

"I don't know. But there's a contract. Seven years."

15

It took him a long time to get back. His legs were wobbly, and twice he took the wrong road. It was only a few miles to the ropeworks, but it seemed to Roddy that now it was on the other side of the world.

Mr. Queed was still gone with the wagons. Roddy saw that as he approached. He expected to find Frank Beasling lurking around like a sentry, waiting to jump out with a hundred questions.

But no one was there as Roddy entered. Most likely Lester had snuck off and Frank was tailing behind to see what trouble he'd get into. Empty, the ropeworks seemed vast and heavy with gloom. Roddy gave a few halfhearted turns to his wheel, making an awful creak. Then he went into the house.

The smell of soup leaked from the kitchen. Sour and slick with some unknown fat floating on top, it held no appeal for him. Earlier, Ivars had given him some gingerbread and handed him a flask of cider. He'd eaten and drunk his fill there with the strange old man and his dark-haired daughter. So, unlike most nights, no hunger drove him to the table and Mother Fecula's foul soups.

He wondered what they were eating back at home. At that very moment, his mother might have been slicing bread fresh from the oven. Or maybe she was making redeye gravy from a big juicy ham.

Roddy pushed those thoughts away. It never did any good to dwell on what he'd lost. For six more years, it would be briny, slimy potato soup with a few bits of bone he might suck for the marrow.

He closed his eyes and thought of the gingerbread Ivars had given him. Was this how they ate in the old country? he wondered. Cakes with sugar icing and sweetmeats? Big flagons of cream and strong cider? Had they sat at a table set with silver and heaped with goose and lamb and beefsteaks? Were there butlers and serving girls and footmen whisking the dishes in from the kitchen?

"Nothing for you tonight!" The old woman's gravelly voice cut through Roddy's daydreams. "The master is eating at the inn. The other boys got their meals before. Nothing for you."

Fecula stood in the doorway with a great tin spoon in one hand. She eyed him as though he'd just committed some terrible crime. "I know where you've been," she growled. "I can smell it on you. Gingerbread. Nice soap that a pretty girl would use." She sniffed at Roddy. "Something else. Rattlesnake. Yes, that's what I smell. Rattlesnake bones."

She waved the spoon as though it were a wizard's wand. "Rattlesnake bones and burnt iron from the sky," she hissed. "I know where you've been, and I know who you've been talking to."

Roddy closed his fist on the little meteorite in his pocket. It got warm faster than a stone would. He felt a little throb of heat pulsing into his fingers.

"You think you're special," Fecula said. Her tongue poked between her lips as she spoke. "Going off with that crazy old man and his girls. But you're just a rope-monkey. Don't you never forget that. You work and you obey and that's all. Nothing special. Nothing blessed. Nothing pretty. Nothing at all."

She made a horrible wet sound deep in her throat, as though she'd swallowed Roddy whole. She waved the spoon again at him, like carving a word in the air. "Nothing," she whispered. And was gone.

16

Alone again, Roddy stood there a long time. It was so quiet with all the other boys gone. How often did he have the house to himself? Perhaps once in a month. No Frank spying on him, waiting for him to make some mistake. No Charlie and Lester trying to coax him into their trouble-making. No Uriah showing him toads and rocks like they were crown jewels. "Look here! Look here!" Uriah would cry, and track Roddy down, because he was the only one who'd pay attention to these foolish treasures. And no Mr. Queed demanding another hour of labor at the wheel.

The others would all be back soon enough, pouring into the house with their loud commotion. But for a little while longer, it was quiet as a church at midnight.

Roddy went outside, out behind the ropeworks to a little rise that looked over the hemp fields. Folks in Pharaoh grew corn and wheat like most others in the valley. But they also planted plenty of hemp, for Mr. Queed's ropeworks could use just about all they grew.

At harvest time, the stalks went up almost twice Roddy's height. Acre after acre of the huge swaying plants. It being early summer, they had a long while to go yet, before they reached their full height. Then the men with the scythes would come, cutting, cutting, cutting for weeks.

That time was both terrible and wonderful for Roddy. Such a powerful smell rising off the fields. Such a dreadful sight as the men swung their sharp blades in the hot sun, like soldiers cutting down innocent people.

And the sound, that was what most troubled Roddy during harvest time. A strange singing came from the fields. It was the whine of sharp steel against living plants. But it was something else too. A far-off wail of sadness.

When he was a little boy, he thought he could understand the noise that the wind-shaken trees made. It sounded like words to him, real language. And he told his mother what the trees were saying. She whipped him for that, saying that was heathen kind of talk. Then he told one of his brothers, "The trees say there's a storm coming," and his brother hit him on the back of the head, as though that could drive such crack-brained ideas out of him.

So he kept more to himself afterward, though he wondered if his parents suspected him of still having those wicked and wayward thoughts. The noise of his mother's spinning wheel sounded like a girl crying. The crackle of the fire might have been a lost soul trying to talk. The chirp of crickets on a sleepy afternoon, and wagon wheels pounding over the dusty road, and even the house creaking as it settled down at night — all of these were trying to say something to Roddy.

And so, when his mother took him aside and told him he'd soon go off to be an apprentice, he was sure it was a punishment. He was bad. He was peculiar. He was, as the preacher said of old King Belshazzar, "weighed in the balance and found wanting." And so he was sent away.

And from then on, until the day before, hearing the crows and feeling he could understand them, he'd been free of those strange, troubling voices.

The noise of the ropeworks had protected him. Ten hours, twelve hours, of the humming and creaking made a blanket of sound that kept away all the others. Arriving there for his first day of work, he had felt as though he were drowning in the noise. But then he'd wondered if that was his parents' plan, to apprentice him out someplace where he would never be troubled by the distant heathen voices again.

Now, standing in the quiet behind the ropeworks, he understood. He might be different, but he wasn't a vile thing. The old king saw something strange and right in him. Perhaps the message the crows brought was simple. Yes, you can hear. Yes, you can understand. Yes, you are the one.

17

Work was awful the next day. Mr. Queed was twice as mean as usual. He shouted curses, and twice rapped his knuckles on Uriah's head, as though to see if anyone were home. "Nottworth, knothead, not a brain in your skull," he growled, when Uriah got one of the lines all tangled up.

"And keep that crank steady," he yelled at Roddy. "Or I'll chain your feet to it and you'll sleep out here too."

During one of their very brief breaks, Charlie explained that Mr. Queed had only gotten half of what he expected for the wagonloads of rope. "Somebody's shipping it over from Buffalo on the canal," he whispered. "So the price has dropped considerable."

"Back to work, you lazy sons of dogs," Mr. Queed shouted, pounding a stick on an old empty barrel. "You'll be here till midnight at the rate you're working."

Roddy grabbed hold of the crank handle, and got the lines

turning again. Mr. Queed set to work braiding and twisting. Uriah and Lester took their places at the hackling combs, grunting in rhythm as they dragged the hemp through the iron teeth. Pulleys squealed. Great wooden spools turned on their creaking axles. Frank paced back and forth, murmuring like cold rain on a rooftop.

The noises all went on, louder and louder, as though battling with each other. But there were no winners in this contest, just a steady rising din.

It hurt Roddy. Not his ears, but some place deeper in him. Yes, the noise was loud enough to rattle the little windowpanes. Yes, he'd have to shout to be heard over it. But it hurt in a different way.

He tried not to let memories of his mother and father rise up. But this noise, it was them somehow. It was shouting him down, not letting his true thoughts have room to live. "Those are heathen voices you hear," his mother had said. "It's the Devil himself talking, if they say to shirk your duty or not work as hard as you can. Work's the only true good thing. Work, and plenty of it."

The crank went round and round. His hands were numb, his arms like dead things still moving.

His term of apprenticeship was seven years. But turning the crank, watching Mr. Queed move up and down the ropewalk, Roddy thought it might as well be forever. He'd get old, gray, and mean as Mr. Queed, and still be there at the crank. The others would move on to new jobs, new places. And he'd still be there, slaving at the crank.

When he first began there, he used to think he was not much better than a mule, doing the same job hour after hour. A mule trudged in circles to turn a grindstone. Or walked a treadmill, mile after mile, but got nowhere. Roddy was no better than that, a prisoner to the crank, though the chains were invisible.

Now it was worse than that. He was not a mule, but a machine. Day by day, week by week, he was more like a little engine. After seven years, he'd have no power of speech, no hopes, no ideas. Just to turn the crank, that was all. Just to make the strands of rope twist and twine. That would be his only reason to live.

A voice cut through these dismal thoughts. Mr. Queed's words were as loud as the pulleys' squeaking. "Silver? You say real silver coin? Not paper notes? True silver?"

Roddy slowed the crank down. Mr. Queed had stopped

moving. Other boys were putting their work aside.

"For which one?" Mr. Queed asked, whining and wheedling like a greedy little child. "You'll pay me now in silver for one little whelp?"

The crank came to a rest. The whole of the ropeworks had stopped. Frank glared at Roddy, as though to say, "Get it moving! Get back to work!" But no one paid any mind to Frank's looks and snarls now.

"Any fair and reasonable price," a girl said.

Roddy stepped away from the crank. Yes, there at the end of the ropewalk was Thea. "My father will pay whatever is right," she said.

And there was King Ivars too. With his strange baggy cloak, and his white beard like a cloud, it seemed wrong for him to be there. Only dirt and hemp fibers, only boy-sweat and the stink of axle grease, should be there, Roddy thought.

Not a king and his beautiful daughter. That was like putting two diamonds into a bucket of slops. "They ought not to be here," Roddy said. Frank told him to shut up. "They should go," Roddy whispered.

"My father has need of a good boy to help us. He'll pay the

complete price for his apprentice papers. Whatever is fair and honest."

"Silver," King Ivars said, holding out a heavy canvas bag.

He'll take Charlie or Lester. They're the biggest. They can do the most work, Roddy thought.

"Which one did you have in mind?" Mr. Queed asked. "Your choice. Any one you want."

Frank and Charlie and Lester had gone up close to the visitors. Even Uriah was sidling toward them.

"There is another boy," Thea said. "He is not so tall as these."

"That one? Down there?" Mr. Queed pointed.

Thea nodded. "Yes, that is him. The one called Roddy."

18

"Boy! Come here!" Mr. Queed shouted.

Roddy went along the ropewalk, following the path Mr. Queed had gone a thousand times. The others stared, and their looks of anger grew more fierce as he approached.

"Why him?" Frank whined. "Why would you want —"

"Shut your mouth!" Mr. Queed cuffed Frank on the side of his head. Then he pointed at Roddy. "Come on, boy. The gentleman wants to buy your papers. Don't you fancy a new master?"

King Ivars was the only one smiling. Even Thea seemed pained by the sight of Roddy trudging toward them. "Him," Ivars said. "Yes. That boy."

"Don't go," Frank muttered as Roddy went by. "You'll regret it."

King Ivars put out his hand and Roddy grasped it, like a grown-up man meeting his friend. "Him. Good boy," the king said in English. Then: "Good silver coins."

"But why?" Frank exploded.

"I told you to shut it!" Mr. Queed yelled. Still, everyone was wondering the same questions. Why Roddy? Why pay so much for a lowly rope-monkey's freedom? What could this boy have that a king would want?

Mr. Queed led them into the house, and told King Ivars to sit down at the big dining room table. Then he disappeared to find Roddy's papers.

"But my mother and father," Roddy said quietly, more to himself than anyone else. "They wanted me here. They found me this situation. They'll be displeased if I go off to some other —"

"My father says you are the one we need," Thea told him. "You understand about the crows. You know this place. You know the Ten Thousand Charms. Rattlesnake bones. Hot iron from the sky. The King of Crows."

Roddy felt himself falling. Not to the floor, as in a faint, but falling on the inside. Thea's words were rushing in like water from some high rocky place. "My parents won't allow it," he whispered.

Mr. Queed returned, with a sheaf of greasy papers. "It's here somewhere, I'm sure."

"Don't you have to tell my mother and father?" Roddy asked.

But Mr. Queed, made frantic by that bag full of silver, was digging through the papers. "It's here, it's here. I know it."

Thea said, "You have to agree, Roddy. You have to say yes. My father can pay the money over to your master. But you have to agree also."

"But why?"

Then Mr. Queed let out a wild whoop and waved a paper at King Ivars. "I knew it! I knew it!" He grabbed for the silver.

"Roddy has to say yes first." Thea, though only his age, was sure and firm as a judge. "He decides one way or the other."

"It's fine, boy. Perfectly. We'll get along without you." Mr. Queed looked like a starving rat who smells delicious food. "Don't worry about a thing here. We'll miss you. But it'll be fine."

Roddy thought of himself at the crank, turning and turning. His parents had sold him to that crank. They traded him for a few dirty bank notes. And now he was worth a bag of silver.

Did Ivars scare him? Yes, of course. The king was strange and old and foreign. He didn't make sense when he talked, and worse, his head was stuffed with bizarre ideas. Did Thea scare him too? Yes, but in a very different way.

"I'll go," Roddy said. And that was all.

Mr. Queed grabbed the bag and stabbed his hand into the pile of money. He didn't look up, even to watch Roddy leave.

But old Mother Fecula appeared as the king and his boy left the house. She came up from the cellar, like a shadow pulling itself free from the deeper darkness. She stared at Roddy with such ugly hate in her eyes, he rushed by the king to get away from her. "You'll be back," Fecula croaked. "You can't get free so easy as all this."

Then she made a noise that could have been a laugh, or a groan, or the snarl of a dying animal.

19

And so Roddy began his new life as the king's boy.

They went directly back to the old Seven house. King Ivars called out to Mina and Nyxie. They stared at Roddy as though he were a nasty, dirty frog brought into some elegant dining room. They didn't groan or say, "Oh Papa, why would you do such a thing?" But it was clear to Roddy that not everyone welcomed him there.

"And let it be so!" King Ivars said, loud and strong, as if talking to a crowd of his subjects. "Let everyone know that this boy is now free!" He waved the apprenticeship papers over the coals in the fireplace.

"He was bound. But now he is released from that bondage." The only time Ivars liked being king of Schatzburg was when he could stand on the balcony of the palace and make such speeches. "As of this day and forever hence, this boy is bound by law to no man. Let it be love, or yearning, or eagerness that binds him to another. Not the words of law or the fear of punishment." King Ivars was pleased with himself for making such a fine speech. And as he dropped the papers into the fire and watched them catch and blaze, he smiled brightly, the flames flickering in his eyes.

Thea told him what her father had said.

Roddy still didn't understand why he was there, what the old king wanted from him.

"There's a room back behind the kitchen," Thea said. "Papa had us fix it up for you."

At that, Mina let out a loud sigh. "He's not a prince," she sniffed. "He's barely civilized enough to wear shoes. I don't see why we have to make such a fuss for a peasant boy."

Thea went on. "I'll show you where you'll sleep."

The room was small, but wonderful. For the first time in his life, Roddy could lie in bed all night without hearing snores or muttered sleep-talk.

There was a window, but it didn't look outside. The kitchen had been added onto the house, and so his little panes faced right at the big fireplace. His bed was made up with a quilt done in strange snaking patterns of black and gold. "Is that from the old country?" he asked.

Thea nodded. "We all worked on it, cutting and piecing. Nyxie was too little to do much, but we let her put in a few stitches. Mina drew the pattern. She has a steady hand. Always steady and sure."

Thea stood awkwardly in the doorway. "It is not very good. Sloppy. Is that the right word? The quilting is zigzag and a little bit terrible." She said this as though it were something ugly and rough. But to Roddy, who'd slept in rough tow sacks and lumpy wool blankets, the quilt was more perfect than sunrise.

Mina stuck her head in. "He could cut some wood for us. Or is that too much to ask such an important visitor?"

"You must excuse her," Thea said. "She is that way to everyone. It has been terribly hard for her, coming to this new place. If we had not needed to flee, Mina would be a crown princess now. There were a half dozen royal boys courting her. Is that how you put it?"

Roddy said, "So your father really was a king?"

"He still is," Thea said sadly. "But he has no kingdom."

Again Mina told Roddy that they needed firewood to make supper.

"It has been hard for all of us. But more so for Mina. She surely does not want to be here."

"And do you?"

"I cried a lot at first." That was all she'd say.

20

Night came like great bands of black cloth winding round and round the old Seven house. They were only a few miles from Pharaoh. Still, it was lonely and silent there. And just beyond the cornfield was the edge of the Bastery Wood. How far it went, Roddy didn't know. But likely it reached all the way to the river.

King Ivars said he was sorry for such a poor evening meal. "My girls are still learning. They never cooked until we came to America." But it was better than anything Roddy had had since leaving home. Bacon and hominy and some field greens cooked with leeks. And a big cup of buttermilk to wash it down.

King Ivars drank beer. One mug, two, and three, till his nose and cheeks were red and his voice a little slurred. He was full of joy. And this was his celebration.

"Ten Thousand Charms," he sang in German, with Nyxie

joining him. She had by far the sweetest singing voice. "Ten thousand secrets for all to see!" Her face shone like a glowing lamp.

"Ten thousand miles around the world, ten thousand locks, one golden key."

The girls drank cider, and they grew merry too. Even Mina joined in when Ivars sang, "Red is roses, black is thorns, white is winter, sound the horns."

Roddy sat by the fire, in a stupor of happiness. Why had Ivars bought his freedom? Why were his feet warm and his belly full? Why did he have a pretty little bed all his own?

He wondered, but not for long. This moment, he knew, would not last forever. Like the cup of cider that Thea passed to him, he could drink it now, or lose his chance.

So he hummed along with their strange German songs. And he kept his feet just close enough to the fire to feel good. And when it was time for bed, he went off, already halfway to dreamland.

He lay there a long time, staring at his candle flame flickering and finally guttering out. It seemed that the light remained though, in his little room. "I'm already dreaming," he whispered. "My eyes are open, and I'm dreaming."

21

Thea stayed up with her father, long past the others. She sat before the fire, staring at the red embers, seeing cities and empires there, towers and castles fall to ruin. She looked into the crimson glow, and she could see across the great ocean. Or perhaps she saw a hundred years into the past. Faces came and went. Fiery armies surged and faded to nothing. And she even heard voices, muttering and hissing and speaking strange tongues.

Was this one of the Ten Thousand Charms? Or were her thoughts all muddled from the strong cider and staying awake so late?

She sat up straighter, cleared her throat. She rubbed her eyes, as if to clear away cobwebs that had blurred her sight. "Papa?" she said. But Ivars was asleep in his chair.

Roddy had gone to bed first. Then Mina had ushered Nyxie off and hadn't come back. So Thea had had a little time alone with her father, quiet and peaceful, watching the embers slowly collapse into themselves.

They'd talked about the old country a little, fond, far-off memories, until Ivars had fallen asleep.

Now darkness was almost complete. Only a faint shimmer of red could be seen in the fireplace.

Thea felt a cold breeze, though she knew the door was closed. She looked over her shoulder, into the shadows rich and purple as a bruise. Someone was there. Someone had joined her. A pair of yellow eyes opened in the darkness, and it seemed that a faint light came out, as from two tiny lanterns.

"It's you again," Thea said. German or English, even Latin, she knew the visitor would understand any tongue. Was she afraid? Of course. But a strange calmness surrounded the fear, like a warm blanket around a shivering child.

"What do you want?"

He didn't answer. He merely fixed her with his fierce yellow eyes.

His name was Scalander, though how Thea knew this, she couldn't have explained. The name had just appeared in her thoughts. Scalander edged closer, and the hearth embers glowed brighter. Even closer, and the coals burst into bright flame.

Thea had a good view of her visitor. Scalander was dark, but not like an African. There was a clay-red hue to his skin. But Thea knew he was not an Indian. She'd never seen such eyes. They were a fiery yellow, like burning sulfur.

"Papa," she whispered. "Papa, wake up." The old king snored on, sprawled out in his chair. She reached to shake him, but Scalander came closer still, and she backed away.

"Don't hurt him," she said, meaning her father.

It wasn't the old king that Scalander had come to see.

"Pretty, pretty, pretty," he hissed. Not like a snake, but like drops of rainwater boiling instantly to steam as they hit red-hot iron.

Thea turned and looked to Roddy's window that faced into this room. The little panes of glass were sheer black. She was alone, all alone, with the visitor.

He held a white bone in one hand, like a king's scepter. He had no crown, but a ring of raised nubs on his bare scalp. He stood, moved his lips as though kissing a phantom, and held the bone above him.

Then the flames rose their highest, reaching and churning. Thea saw the red writhing of the flames, yet she felt no increase in warmth. Perhaps, she thought, this was just a reflection of

some other, far-off flames. A picture of a fire in a charmed looking glass. In that other world, she thought, the heat must be terrible to feel. But here, it was cold as the night sky.

The flames increased till Thea could barely stand to look into the brightness. They flooded the room and, like a brilliant full moon blotted by sudden clouds, were instantly gone. With the flames went Scalander. And with Scalander went Thea's thoughts, circling down into dreamless sleep.

22

The next morning, Mina was up first to make the cooking fire. Nyxie joined her, and went out to fetch water. Roddy was awake too, but lay in his warm, soft, serene new bed. He listened to the girls whisper and rustle in the next room. He tried to make out whose voice was whose. Nyxie dropped a tin plate, and Mina hissed like a furious tomcat.

Roddy rolled over, easing his face into the goose-down pillow. Back at Mr. Queed's factory, the other boys had already been at work for hours. And here Roddy lay, lazy as August sunshine.

He felt only a tiny flicker of guilt. Why, again he asked himself, had King Ivars bought his freedom? But that thought came and went quickly. The comfort of the bed was like rain and warmth to a newly planted seed. And Roddy could already feel the changes happening inside him.

Soon enough there came a tap on his door, and he rose for breakfast. Thea and her father weren't up yet.

He had cornmeal mush and strong coffee with as much cream as he wanted. Mina worked a pair of tin snippers on the sugar loaf when Roddy asked for some. He dropped the chunk of gritty sweetness into his coffee and watched the tiny bubbles rise. Sugar in coffee, he thought. This isn't paradise, but it'll do till I get there.

Shortly, he was outside, looking around the old Seven house. There were fields and pastures in front. Likely Ivars would want Roddy to start clearing away the scrub that had sprung up since the land was last tilled. This would be hard, sweaty work, but after a year in the rope factory, it seemed like a blessing, not a curse.

Out back, the Bastery Wood grew in closer than Roddy had thought. Even in bright morning sunshine, the forest loomed dark and dense, like a great wall of living shadow. He'd heard the other boys talk of the game still roaming those woods, deer and rabbit mostly, and bear and wolf too, if the stories were true.

At home, Roddy had done a little hunting. But the woods

near his home had been logged and plowed before he was born. What remained were just little patches, in deep gullies and other out-of-the-way places. The Bastery Wood was different. He knew Charlie and Lester liked to exaggerate, but they both claimed it ran back for miles, as deep and trackless as it had been when the white people first came.

Once, in Pharaoh, a man had appeared on Main Street, shouting and claiming he had captured the king of all bears. Of course he wanted folks to pay for the privilege of seeing this Lord of Monsters. He talked through a long trumpet, loud and shrill, and soon he had a few dozen people lined up to enter his little tent.

The man had chosen his time well, late on Saturday. The streets of Pharaoh were full, and even the rope-monkeys were in town with a penny or two to waste on amusement.

All except Frank, they paid their fee and filed into the tent. "You're all fools, every one of you!" Frank announced. "Mr. Queed will hear about this."

Still the boys went, and saw the King of Woodland Beasts. At first, Roddy hung back, truly afraid of the snarling and thrashing. But then laughter began among the oohs and aahs. It wasn't a real bear at all, but a man in a moth-eaten costume.

Mostly it was bear fur, Roddy supposed. But there were places it had been patched with the skins of goats and rabbits. The sewn-up spots looked like scars. The holes looked like old wounds.

The man in the bear suit roared and lunged about. The man with the voice trumpet told a hundred fascinating lies about the bear. And when the show was over, all agreed it was worth the price, even if it had all been a shoddy trick.

Now Roddy stared at the massy forest wall and wondered if real bears lurked about in there. The rattlesnake bones King Ivars had shown him before surely weren't fake. But they might have been a hundred years old, from back when the Iroquois were the only ones there.

A single crow cawed, off in the distance. A minute later came the answer, from closer by. Roddy scanned the skies. A few black flecks moved against the blue. Another burst of noise came, raucous as soldiers on the battlefield.

They were coming, all of them. Roddy didn't so much see it as feel their approach. A thousand crows, and a thousand more swarming from all four directions.

The Parliament of Crows was meeting one last time. First the lone voices and the far-off answers. Then small flocks and bigger squadrons, till the sky was spattered with countless ragged black marks.

In minutes, the clamor was so loud it hurt Roddy's ears. He stood in the open. But there were trees here and there on the farmstead, big old oaks and elms. Soon enough, these were heavy with crows, every branch drooping under the sudden weight.

The house door was thrown back and out came King Ivars, carrying his heavy book. Thea appeared at the door too, in her nightdress. Her hair was uncombed, unbound, a wild flow of darkness. She called for her father to come back. The old king hurried to where Roddy stood, shouting words that he couldn't understand.

23

Thea watched from the shelter of the house. She was afraid, trembling, in fact, from fear. Yes, she'd been out in the fields before, when the crows were gathering. But this time, the number of birds was ten times greater, and the black noise was already loud enough to drown out her shouts. "Papa! Get back in the house."

And still the birds came on.

She'd heard a traveling preacher in Pharaoh, just the month before, tell about the end of the world. "There shall be signs in the heavens!" Preacher Dow had shouted from the pulpit. And the people sat rigidly on the stiff wooden benches, hanging on every word. "Look to the skies, if you would see the end coming nigh!" Much of what the preacher said made no sense to Thea. These people here in York State were so filled with strange beliefs, strange movements of the spirit. Back at home in Schatzburg, church was a calm, sleepy affair with beautiful music. The choir and the big pipe organ and the tolling bells. The altar boys in their gorgeous robes, like drowsy angels. And stained glass and the smell of burning incense. Not here though, in this rough and unfinished place. Church was as raw as the winter weather. Bare white walls, shouting songs, preachers overcome with joy and dread.

Some of that feeling now filled her as she watched her father and Roddy stand in the middle of the swirling black storm.

They were talking together, pointing and turning slowly around, as though visitors to some hall of wonders. She wanted to join them, but fear had put a cold chain around her heart.

"In the old Hebrew times," Preacher Dow had wailed at the congregation, "locusts filled the skies like black thunderclouds. How much more terrible will it be when the end-times come?"

"Papa!" Thea shouted. Her voice was like one raindrop swallowed up in a raging sea. "Papa, please!"

Nyxie was behind her, clutching at her arm. "Make him come back," her sister whimpered.

"He can't hear me."

Mina stood in the doorway now also. No tears, no trembling. But she too was sorely afraid.

Suddenly a line of crows, straight and long, like a great spear, flew across the sky. King Ivars shouted, but it wasn't fear that gripped him. He pointed, and Roddy nodded eagerly.

With that, Thea bolted from the house. She ran across the stubbly field, across the little pasture. "Papa, come back to the house!"

"Terrible! Wonderful!" her father said in English.

Just as Thea reached her father, the crows rose in one enormous black mass. They flew upward and blotted out the sun. Thea and Roddy and Ivars were in shadow suddenly, swallowed in cold, moving darkness.

And just as suddenly, the shadow passed, flying northward into the Bastery Wood.

Roddy was breathing like a runner who'd gone a dozen miles. King Ivars shut his eyes and pressed his book to his chest. And Thea held on to them both, to keep from collapsing.

It was a long time before anyone spoke.

24

Roddy cut stove wood that day, and climbed up on the roof to fix a leak. He dug a little in the old kitchen garden, finding in the tangled weeds some carrots and turnips from last year.

His thoughts, however, were always on the crows, their noise and black flight northward.

After the crows fled, he came back to the house with King Ivars and spoke as best he could with the old man. Thea translated. Mina interrupted now and then. And even Nyxie put in a few words. What was happening? Why had the crows come together a last time, and then fled just as suddenly? The only thing that Roddy knew for certain was that the crows had finished their parliament that morning. Their business was done.

"Nord, sud, ost, west," King Ivars said, pointing to a map he'd drawn. The house was a little box. The town of Pharaoh, near the bottom of the page, was a sketchy circle. The Genesee River went straight up and down. And the edge of the Bastery Wood lay like a great shadowy wall to the north.

"Nord," Ivars said, tapping his finger at the top of the page. He said something more in German.

Thea asked him to repeat it, then said, "He gets confused sometimes." There was anger now in her voice, and it was directed at Roddy. "His mind gets turned around and upside down. When he gets all stirred up or sees something new and strange, he forgets he has come to America. Or it all gets blurry in his mind."

He patted Roddy on the shoulder, like a father comforting his son, and went to his room. They heard the bed cords creaking, and soon the soft whistling of Ivars's snores.

"He gets tired out by too much agitation," Thea said. "Is that the right word? Excitement is not so good for his heart. He should not be out there. It is wrong for him. Bad. We all should not be here." There were tears now in her eyes. "This is not our place. We should be home." She meant the old country. "Wrong and bad. Everything is wrong." It seemed she was blaming Roddy. But what had he done? "We will never see the castle again, or St. Gottfried's, or our poor mama's tomb." She sniffed back the tears, hard and angry. She pointed at Roddy with a trembling hand.

"This is a bad place. Terrible. It will kill him, I just know it. He will go off looking for some charms or wonders and never come back. And then what will happen to us? We should not be here. It is not our place."

With that she fled from the house.

25

Bursting into the daylight, she remembered the black clouds of crows. But the skies were quiet now, empty and still. She came up short, now with the broad blue of morning stretched over her head.

They were gone, all of them. Back where they'd come from.

Though warm sunshine bathed the land, and early morning peace had returned, Thea was uneasy. The crows were gone. Yes, that was certain. But something wrong remained.

Perhaps it was all inside her. For the first time since coming to Pharaoh, she let herself feel the homesickness. Right then, she knew, in far-off Schatzburg, the old wonderful life went on. Perhaps the church bells were calling people to gather. Bakers set out their cakes, shiny with sugar icing. A street vendor was singing and showing his wares: "Cinnamon! Ginger! Nutmeg and cloves!" Girls went to shops and giggled about how they'd look in such beautiful gowns. Boys played at being soldiers, shouting and making bugle sounds with their cupped hands. And butchers hung long ropes of sausage out to ripen in the sun.

Right then, across the ocean, her old life was going on without her. In the castle, some stranger sat on the throne. And perhaps this stranger's daughter slept in the bed that had once been Thea's.

She missed the old life of balls and fine music, feast days and bonfires that burned all night. She missed seeing her father in his court robes, pottering about the castle with his crown askew. Would she rather be home, as a princess of Schatzburg? Of course. But what grieved her most was not losing the finery and pomp, but the simple sense of home.

This western backland of York State was not so terrible. Indeed, when the weather was good, it could be delightful to wander the woods and pasturelands. But it wasn't hers. She didn't know the beasts and birds. The food was strange, and even the sunshine felt different.

Thea walked down a meandering path. Weeds had overtaken the fields there, unplowed for years. Then she passed through the shade of some beech trees. The path took her over a little ridge and into deepening woodland.

She barely noticed though. Her thoughts kept winding back to the old country. Food and drink, music and church, the sound of her own language spoken by hundreds and thousands — she missed all of this. But stronger by far was her longing to see her mother's face again.

That, of course, could never be. She was lying in the beautiful marble tomb at St. Gottfried's. She'd taken the road to heaven, as her father said. And they would not meet until Thea also had left this world for the next.

Again, the old raw anger filled Thea. Why had her mother gone away? Sickness or no, heaven-bound or not, she'd abandoned her girls. Yes, her papa was a good man. But he was lost too often in his studies and strange ideas. Thea wanted her mother, right then and right there. The ache was so fierce in her chest that it pushed everything away. Her breath, the beating of her heart, they were gone. All that remained, as Thea wandered, was the pain.

Through a veil of hot tears, she went along the path.

She was out of the sunlight now. The trees were older here, fat around and furry with moss. The ground was soft with dead leaves. A different kind of silence now surrounded her, close and heavy.

Wiping her eyes, she stopped and looked around. For the first time she wondered who walked along this path, keeping the weeds down. The Seven house had been empty for years. And the place wasn't close to anyone else's farm. Why did this trail, which seemed to head straight into the woods, stay clear?

To one side, at the bottom of a slope, was a little creek. It was no rushing silver stream, but a silent line of dark ooze. Careful now, steadying herself by grabbing roots and saplings, she eased herself down to the creek bed.

The smell was rich and rank, as the sun never reached there to dry out the ground. Thea stood and watched the quiet black current. Only by listening closely could she hear the faint sound.

A flash of motion caught her eye. She crouched closer. Another darting of the shadow. She knelt, not caring that her dress would get soaked, and there was a tiny creature. He was a shimmery black-red, with brilliant yellow eyes. In Germany, the name was "Molch," but here in America, Thea thought, it was "newt."

He stared up at her with those brilliant eyes like two drops of molten gold. She brought her face closer, expecting him to run. But he was perfectly still. Usually, a creature this small, faced by the hugeness of a human, would be frozen with fear. But Thea sensed none of that in the newt.

"Where did you come from?" she whispered.

Still, he didn't move.

"Why do you not show any fear?"

Slowly, she put her hand down to his level. Surely he'd scoot off now to hide in the rotted leaves and shining black mud. But no, he took a few steps toward her, then, with a slight nod, climbed into her hand.

She lifted him to eye level. Only then did she see the tiny, crownlike ring of bumps around the top of his head.

"Herr Molchkonig," she said, then thought, No, this is America. He doesn't understand German. "Hail the King of the Newts!"

She expected him to nod back. Or even stand up on his back feet and bow. He did neither, just stared at her with those liquid yellow eyes.

"Why no fear?" she asked again.

Then she wondered where her own bad feelings had vanished to. She could surely call the homesickness up from its hiding place. But right then, it was gone. She could be angry again at her father for bringing the strange boy into their house. However, she didn't feel it anymore. She knew soon enough she'd feel the ache for her mother. Still, that awful longing was far away now.

A third time, she asked the newt why he wasn't afraid. And a third time he gave no answer but the look in his bright uncanny eyes.

She set him down and headed up the bank to the trail. All the way, she felt the newt staring at her. And going back the way she came, she sensed his gaze too, though no matter how fast he ran, he couldn't keep up with Thea. Still, he was with her somehow, watching.

26

Mr. Simeon Queed sat alone in his house, counting the money he'd gotten for Roddy. He'd been through the stacks of silver twice already. But how he loved the feel of the cold coins between his fingers. How he loved the glint of candlelight on the bright metal.

Mr. Queed had heard the rumors in town. The old stranger was rich beyond imagining. He had the power to conjure up cartloads of silver. That's what some folks said. He was a heathen Catholic, with a house full of pagan icons and strange books. That's what the Reverend Johnstone said. And the three girls were really ancient hags, witch-sisters who used old-world magic to make themselves appear young.

These stories might be for fools and ninnies. Mr. Queed certainly didn't believe most of this taletelling. But the little mountain of silver coins was real. There was no question about that. The old bearded one had huge wealth. Silver by the bagful. Perhaps gold too. He was supposedly a banished king. Might he still have a crown? A scepter encrusted with jewels?

The thought of so much wealth made Mr. Queed weak and dizzy. There, out at the old Seven place, was a fortune for the taking.

He held a large silver coin to the candlelight. On one side was the face of a queen, proud as a lion. On the other side was a royal crest and words in Latin.

Like a baby fascinated by a new toy, he put the coin in his mouth. The taste was bad, the feel was strange, yet he left it there a moment. "More," he said, with the coin still on his tongue. "I want more. I want it all."

Just then he heard a rustling sound from behind. He spun and growled, "What are you doing here?" The coin fell out of his mouth. It hit the floor and rolled into the darkness. "I told you not to —"

"Doesn't matter what you told me," old Mother Fecula said. "Not your place to give me orders."

She cooked for him, and cleaned, and washed the clothes. She stood by silently as he lectured the boys about right living. He owned the house and the ropeworks. Still, he never felt he was truly the master there.

"What do you want?"

Wealth was nothing to her. She slept in a tiny, windowless room at the back of the kitchen. Her clothes were old and patched a hundred times. She was satisfied to sweat over cookpots and stacks of dirty dishes.

Power was nothing. She needed no servants nor lackeys doing her will. She had no desire to give orders and watch a dozen people scurry about at her whim.

Good food? No. Whiskey or chewing tobacco? No. Music and dancing? No.

"The girl," Fecula said. "I want the girl."

He knew which one she meant. All three were pretty. But Mina held herself too proudly. Her fine princess nose was raised a bit too high in the air. And the young one, Nyxie, was still a little child, playing with dolls.

"The middle one," Mr. Queed said. "The bright one. The one called Thea."

"That's right," Mother Fecula hissed. "I want the pretty one with the soft brown eyes."

"Are they really princesses?" Mr. Queed asked.

"You've seen the silver. You've heard there's a hundred times more in the old man's trunks."

"But why would such people come here? All the way from the old country to live in a ramshackle old farmhouse in the heart of nowhere."

"There's more here than pigs and wheat and hemp fields, and you know it. There's more than backwater fools and crazy preachermen. There's something wild and strange breeding here. And King Ivars has a nose for such things. A very very good nose."

"Is he really a king? Is this royal silver?" Mr. Queed held up a handful of coins and let them spill to the tabletop.

"He bought your boy, didn't he? He knew which one. He bought the Seven house. He knew it was the right place to settle." She sneered at him. "What do you care, as long as it's pure silver? King of a nation, or king of fools. Or both. Why should you care where the money comes from?"

Mr. Queed scowled, but said nothing.

"So be it. Now I have work to do. A man's work is from sun to sun. But a mother's work is never done." She'd said these words so many times, reciting them was like breathing. "Now you keep in mind what I said. I want the pretty one with the soft brown eyes."

And with that, she shuffled back to the kitchen.

27

King Ivars took Roddy hunting the next day. Not for deer or squirrel, but for more signs and wonders.

Nyxie wanted to go along. She begged and wheedled and squeezed out a few false tears. But her father would not budge. "When your English is better," he said. "Not now. I need Thea to translate."

"It doesn't matter, Papa. She'll do fine," Thea said. She wanted nothing to do with such hunting and wandering. The boy Roddy seemed to stir up bad omens: The massing of the crows. The black man with yellow eyes who had come a few nights ago. And even the little king of newts the day before. Hours after seeing him, Thea felt the tiny creature was still watching her.

"Take Nyxie. She wants to go, Papa."

"You do as you're told," the old king said. "You're not so grown-up as you think you are."

She glared at Roddy, resentment curdling in her like milk going bad on a warm day. "Let him learn some German, the dummkopf," she said, pointing at Roddy. Even he knew this meant "fool."

But her father ignored this, nodding toward the door. "We're going. All three of us. You and Roddy and me."

He told Mina to watch over her little sister, and set out for the big flat-topped hill to the east of the house. "Indian mound," he said, then gestured to Thea. "Tell him. People say it's an Indian burial mound, and we're going there to see."

King Ivars brought some of his strange measuring instruments with him. When they reached the hill, he aimed a little brass device at the sun, then swung around in a circle.

He muttered in German and made some notes in his book.

"What is he saying?" Roddy asked.

Thea didn't answer. She was standing at the edge of the hill, looking off toward the Bastery Wood. You could drop the whole kingdom of Schatzburg into the forest, with plenty of room left over. This place, this New World, was so huge, Thea thought. It went on west farther than anyone could calculate or understand.

Her father said, "Over here," and Thea joined him. There was a circle of stones just poking out of the weeds. It might have been the foundation of a little house, or some great pit for fires.

"Dig," Ivars said, pointing to the shovel Roddy carried. "There."

Roddy turned over a few lumps of the sandy earth.

"No. Over here," Ivars said. Thea translated, and Roddy set to work making a little excavation.

"What are we looking for?" he asked.

Thea shrugged. "You tell me. You are the one who draws the crows and tells them to be silent."

Ivars sifted some of the dirt through his fingers, looking closely. Shaking his head, he took Roddy by the arm and led him to a new place.

This went on for an hour or two, wandering around the crest of the hill, digging, poking, making notes.

Finally, Ivars said in German, "Enough for today. I need to look at my books again before we do any more digging." He was disappointed and getting tired.

Thea helped him climb down the side of the hill, and they

walked arm in arm back toward the house. Roddy lagged behind. He swung the shovel lazily in the weeds. He kicked a rock off to one side and followed it, to kick it again.

"Look!" he shouted. "What's this?"

28

"Papa is tired. We need to get him home for a nap." Thea watched wearily, as her father joined Roddy in a low patch of weeds.

"Is it anything?" Roddy asked.

The old man didn't know the words, but he understood the question.

Roddy held up a small circlet of rusted iron.

"It is just the hoop from an old bucket," Thea said. "Toss it away. We need to get Papa back home. He is tired."

But her father had put down his books and was holding the iron ring with both hands. "Eine Krone."

Thea sighed. "He says it is a crown," she told Roddy.

There were little holes all the way around the iron ring. Ivars pointed and said these were the places where jewels had been.

"Papa, don't be foolish. It's from an old bucket, and that's where the nails went through. It's an old piece of trash."

Ivars wouldn't listen. Thea was truly worried now, that her father was losing all his senses. He'd always been excited about his books and specimens and collections of strange things. But Thea had never seen this look on his face. "Eine Krone," he said, lifting the circle toward the sun.

She thought he was going to place it on his own head. But no, he stepped toward Roddy and fit it on him, as though crowning him.

Roddy stood there in his shabby clothes with the old rusty ring on his head. It all might have been a childish game. King of the hill. King of fools. King of the rope-monkeys.

Ivars nodded gravely. He bowed stiffly to Roddy and said something Thea didn't catch.

"Enough of this!" she shouted. "We need to get him back." And Roddy, shocked out of his daze, finally agreed. Each taking an arm of the old man, Thea and Roddy ushered him home.

29

Roddy found a hiding place out behind the house, a little broken-down shack in a clump of scraggly bushes. The boards of the walls were falling off, and the roof was mostly gone.

But it was a private place where no one would bother him. No crazy old men muttering in strange languages. No princesses with their noses high in the air, like Mina. No silly prattling little girls, such as Nyxie. And no flashes of anger, as he got now from Thea.

He sat there in the sun-striped shadows, holding the iron ring. A crown? That was pure foolishness. Still, just for a moment, as Ivars'd placed it on his head, he'd felt something different in himself. Maybe he wasn't just a poor dirty apprentice. For just a moment, he had been royal and regal. "Prince Roddy," he whispered to himself.

He heard the house door open and saw Thea come out with

a clay pitcher. She went to the well and grabbed the long wooden sweep that dipped the mossy old bucket into the depths.

Her sleeves were pulled up and rolled, and her long dress was hoisted and belted to keep it from dragging in the mud. Still, she looked like a princess to Roddy.

Mina's haughty contempt he could stand. He was used to the rich and proud looking down on him. But Thea's anger was ten times worse. It wasn't *his* idea to come there, he wanted to shout at her. It wasn't *his* father whose thoughts were getting more and more muddled. *He* didn't tell crazy stories and expect others to believe them.

Thea filled her pitcher, but didn't go directly back. She turned slowly in a full circle, as though listening.

Roddy was well hidden. Still, he crouched a little lower. Her anger was already bad enough without her finding out he was spying on her.

Thea poured a little water on her hands and smoothed back her hair. The sun was bright and noonday hot. She wet her hands again, then rubbed them on her face and arms.

If I could have a picture, Roddy thought, it would be this.

Thea standing there with her eyes closed, feeling the sun and the warm wind on her face. At peace. Most times she was so worried about her father. And that worry turned into anger. But this was her true self, Roddy thought. Calm and still and beautiful.

30

Stroking the few tangled whiskers that hung from her chin, old Mother Fecula waited for her son.

Darkness lay heavy as a flood. The town of Pharaoh, three hours past midnight, was still and empty.

Fecula sat on a wooden bench, facing the Methodist church. She looked up at the steeple, which jutted into the black heavens. On either side were two great elm trees, standing like sentinels guarding the church.

Not a light shone in any window. All of Pharaoh was asleep. All except old Fecula, and her shadow-black son.

He appeared suddenly.

"You. Diamonds and dirt. You. King of Carrion. You. Best and beast." The old woman said these words as though speaking a spell. To conjure her visitor to fullness? To make him real enough to touch?

She got up and kissed him on the forehead. "So the crows finally made their choice?"

He nodded gravely. He raised his hand, and only then did she see the bone scepter. It shone brilliantly white, though no light of lantern nor moon touched it.

"My boy, my darling young boy. You'll soon have everything you want. Your crown now. And your queen soon."

Almost no one in Pharaoh had really seen Scalander. But they'd all heard the rumors, all whispered the stories back and forth. Some called him a "ghost," a dead spirit still walking the earth. Some claimed he was a half-breed, part Seneca and part runaway slave. Indeed, there were such people in this section of York State. For the mysterious Underground Railroad ran here, like a ghost train carrying lost souls to heavenly freedom.

Fecula had even heard the boys at the ropeworks say he was one of the ancient people, the last of the old race that lived there before even the Indians. There was a missionary who passed through town once, one of Holy Joe Smith's followers. And he talked about the Lamanites, the people who supposedly lived right there in the Genesee Valley many thousands of years back. Frank Beasling, the old woman knew, thought of her son this way.

But they were all wrong. He was just Scalander, her one and only beloved son.

She held his hand. She kissed him again, as a mother would kiss her baby. "The crows have gathered and given their consent. Yes? Yes?" Scalander nodded. "We've waited so long. A royal bride finally has come, and the crows have said their happy yes."

Fecula beamed at her son, proud of him, happy for him.

"You'll have your pretty pretty pretty soon enough."

Scalander smiled, and bright yellow light poured from his eyes.

31

King Ivars was sick that day, and stayed in bed. "He has a brain fever. Is that what you call it?" Thea asked.

"I don't know about such things," Roddy said. "You should have the doctor. Do you want me to go into town for him?"

Thea shook her head. "Papa will not have such things. Back at home, he never had the doctor. 'We have better medicine than leeches and mercury plasters,' he said. And then he would study his books, reading and muttering for hours."

Just saying these words stirred up awful feelings in Thea. Her mother had been lost, she was sure, because her father would not call in the doctors. The king of a country, with all the wealth he could ever need. And yet he refused to bring in a doctor to save his beloved wife.

Thea shook her head, as though to cast out these thoughts. And worse, the anger and pain they called up in her.

"This place is bad," she murmured. "We should not be

here. It is not good for Papa." She pointed to Roddy and raised her voice. "I want you to promise me you will not let him wander all over. It will surely make him sicker."

"He's my master now," Roddy said. "I must do what he tells me."

"You have no master. He bought your papers and burnt them. You did not sign any new contracts. You are free. You do not have to be here. You can leave anytime."

Roddy said, "No. That's not right. He bought me —"

"He bought your papers and he burnt them up. You are free."

"But he's my new master."

"Listen to me, Roddy. Listen close," Thea said. "You have no master. You can walk out the door right now and go back to your people. Where was it? Rector's Ford? Is that where your mother and father are?"

"Yes, but what about —"

"Nothing!" she shouted. "No master! No papers!" She grabbed his hands, squeezing them tight. "Papa is sick, and he will only get sicker with all this wandering and searching and excitement. I want you to go away."

"But he's been kind to me. How can I just walk off?"

"The most kindness, the biggest good, is for you to leave here right now. Today. If you love my papa, then you will do what is best for him. He needs rest and no more agitation."

She could see the sorrow in Roddy's face. A few days of peace and happiness, only to be sent away. "You do not have to go back to the ropeworks. You are not an apprentice anymore. You can see your mother and father again."

"I don't think," Roddy whispered, "they want to see me."

"Surely your own parents —"

"No. They sent me away. They don't want me back. I thought I could live here, serve your father, help you girls. I thought I had a place here." He pulled his hands free from hers and bolted out of the house.

She called for him, but he was gone like a gust of wind.

"Roddy!" She stood in the doorway. Already he was too far to hear her voice.

32

Fast and unthinking, he sped down the path. Back where they'd been the day before. Up the hill where he'd dug and King Ivars had sifted the loose earth.

Bent over puffing, Roddy stood on the hilltop. It wasn't till he'd caught his breath that he saw how dark and low the sky had become. Steely black clouds poured eastward like a vast ocean current.

A storm was coming. Anybody could see that. He'd be drenched if he stayed there. Even if he turned back right then, the rain would surely catch him, soak him to the bone.

Way off he saw the sudden glow of lightning. It came and went, barely visible in the surging storm clouds.

Already he heard a far-off rumble.

Surely he should find shelter. "Go on back," he told himself. Still, he stood on the hilltop, watching, waiting for the storm to hit.

Charlie Near had told him of seeing a boy hit by lightning. "I wasn't so far away. I saw the whole thing. It was the boy who worked the crank before you. They all get hurt bad. It's like a curse." Frank Beasling said this was all lies to scare the new boy. But Charlie told the story so well, Roddy couldn't help but believe it.

"He was standing out in the hemp field, and it was early spring. That's what made it so strange. You never see lightning in March, but there it was, cutting up the sky. And no matter what we said he wouldn't come back. So one bolt hit a big old oak not far away, and I swear it started burning even in the rain. And this boy wouldn't move. It was like he'd been caught by a snake's gaze. What do you call it? Mesmerized. And he couldn't move for looking up at the sky. So he stood there, and the second thunderbolt came cracking out of the heavens. And I swear he was turned to a skeleton in a flash. One minute he was just an ordinary boy and the next he was nothing but bones. I saw it. I swear! The skeleton stood there a minute, all together. Then another clap of thunder hit and the bones all tumbled down to the ground like a load of sticks."

Roddy was never sure if he should believe Charlie's stories. He certainly told some that were made up. But since the gathering of the crows, since Roddy had left the ropeworks, it seemed that anything might be possible.

So there he stood with the rain spattering his face and the sky closing down around him. The lightning was much clearer now, jagged blue-white slices in the sky.

Maybe Charlie was right and the crank-boy was always cursed. Maybe it was simple fate. He got sold away first because his parents didn't need him or want him. He got assigned to the crank because he was the lowliest of all the rope-monkeys. King Ivars picked him because Ivars was a crazy addle-brained old man.

And soon enough, he'd get blasted by lightning, and that would be the end. A little pile of white bones that even the coons and skunks wouldn't notice.

Another bolt struck much closer. He felt the blow up through his feet and legs. "The next one, the next one," he murmured.

He'd show Thea. When the storm was over, she'd come out looking for him. And wouldn't she feel bad, poison-bad, when she found out she'd driven him to this?

The next lightning bolt didn't hit him. Nor the one after that. His ears were ringing from the thunder. His hair was slicked down to his scalp. His eyes were blurry from the rain and the brilliant flashes. But he was still there. And still alive.

The thunder ground around him like huge millstones, and he shouted into the noise, "Here I am! Come on! Here I am!"

This felt good to Roddy, like the time he'd gotten sick after eating a half dozen green apples. It all came out. The apples then, and the words now. "Go on and hit me! Try it and see. Right here. I'm not afraid. Hit me and see if I care!"

He shouted and he waved his fist. However, the storm had better targets than a sopping wet rope-monkey that day. It didn't see Roddy or hear him.

And at last it was clear he would live to face another day. The lightning dwindled away. The black clouds passed over, toward the Bastery Wood. The wind dropped, and Roddy was still alive.

He felt like a little knight who'd challenged a huge, fire-spitting dragon. Soaked through and exhausted, still he'd won. He hadn't run away. He hadn't backed down.

Now the remains of the storm were swirling above the blackness of the Bastery Wood. From this high spot on the hilltop, he saw the shreds of clouds, the mists and last flickers of lightning, dwindle above the forest.

Then it was quiet, still as midnight.

From the hilltop, Roddy could see a long distance in every direction. He looked toward the east, where the old Seven house stood. A tiny figure was inching along the path to the house. But it wasn't coming from town. No, it was approaching from the opposite way, from the great Bastery Wood.

33

Old Mother Fecula walked with a cane. She'd come a long way, and her legs hurt. Her feet hurt too, and her hand from clutching the head of her cane. In her other hand was a basket made from woven oak strips.

The ground was wet but not muddy. The rain had come and gone so quickly, like a tantrum that shakes a little child and then vanishes. By the time Fecula reached the Seven house, the sun was out and the ground was steaming.

She knocked on the door with the head of her cane. From inside, she heard girlish voices. She knocked again, three loud raps.

Thea opened the door and met the old woman's gaze. Yes, Fecula thought, she's the one. Just as my darling boy had said. The pretty one with the soft brown eyes.

"Yes, what is it?" the girl said. Her voice had a little trace of the old country, the "w" buzzing like a "v."

"I come in the service of Mr. Simeon Queed," the old woman said. She tried to smile, but it felt wrong, awkward, false.

"Yes?"

"I've come a long way, my dear. A long way for these old legs. May I come in?"

Thea opened the door wide and ushered Fecula into the main room. A fire was burning low, under a big black kettle. The other two girls were there. They put down their work to stare at the visitor.

"Who is it, Thea?" the older one said.

"My name is Mother Fecula," she said, before Thea could answer. "Mr. Simeon Queed has asked me to come out and make sure the boy has gotten settled. He's not here now?"

The girls looked uncomfortably at each other.

Finally Thea said, "He got angry and ran off."

"I hope nothing's wrong," Fecula said, trying to sound helpful.

Silence was her answer.

"I brought something good for the boy. He always liked this kind of sweet. Poppy seeds and maple sugar." Fecula opened her basket and took out a half dozen little brown cakes. "One for each of you. I'm sure the boy won't mind sharing."

Nyxie came over and grabbed a cake. But Thea told her to put it down. Nyxie whined. Thea was firm. "Not now. Later on."

"But it looks so good!"

"Do as you're told," Mina said.

"But you don't know where the boy is?"

"His name is Roddy," Thea said.

"Of course, of course. You don't know where our old friend Roddy has gotten to?"

From the back of the house came King Ivars's voice. "Who's there?"

"It's an old lady," Nyxie shouted back. "And she's brought us some cakes."

"Our father," Thea explained, "has not been feeling so well."

The sound of feet shuffling and muttered German words came from the room where he rested. Mina went to get him back into bed.

"What is it you want with Roddy?" Thea asked.

"Just to give a greeting and wish him well from his old friends." She took hold of Thea's hand, squeezed and pulled her closer. "You certainly are a pretty one," she whispered.

"How would you like to come to Pharaoh and meet some of the folks in town?"

"Yes, can we go?" Nyxie piped up.

"Maybe sometime." Thea was trying to be polite, but she clearly wanted Fecula to be gone. Twisting her arm, she tried to get out of the old woman's grasp. "Papa is not feeling well. Perhaps when he is better."

Fecula leaned in close, staring into the girl's eyes. Yes, indeed, she thought. My darling boy was right. She's the one. My boy shall have his queen soon enough.

The girl jerked her hand free and said, a little too loudly, "My papa has been very ill. You need to come back another time."

"But can't we go into town for a visit?" Nyxie asked, sulking.

"Another time. Now, please," Thea said, gesturing to the open door. "I need to see about my papa."

Fecula made a little curtsy and left. "Yes, yes, yes," she whispered.

Perhaps a half mile away, the boy was hurrying down the path to the house. But Fecula went the other way, toward the woods, toward the dark places where her darling son would be found.

34

Sitting around the table for the evening meal, the girls were in a somber mood. All three were worried about their father. But they each had their own burden. Nyxie was furious that she wasn't allowed to eat the cakes Fecula had brought. Mina's longing for the old days and the old ways was stronger than ever. All she could talk about was balls they'd been to and handsome officers they'd seen. Thea's burden was simpler. She felt guilty for driving Roddy away that morning.

He had come back after Mother Fecula's visit. And Thea had tried to be more kindly toward him. Still, he said almost nothing as they ate.

Thea brought some soup to her father's room. She broke up biscuits and softened them in the broth. He's like a baby now, Thea thought. We have to watch him all the time. His breathing had calmed down, but he was still weak, and little that he said made any sense.

Roddy went out to cut firewood after supper. With only a nod for good night, he came in and went straight to bed. Nyxie sang a sad song of the old country, sniffling back tears. Mina, for once, didn't scold or order her around. As the sun was just disappearing in the west, she said, "Come on, Nyxie. It's time for bed."

After Thea had washed the dishes and cleaned the table, she sat awhile thinking about the old woman. The little cakes were still uneaten, on a plate by the hearth. Why had she told Nyxie no? The woman was strange and unpleasant. But why turn away such a neighborly gift?

A terrible feeling. That's all she could point to. It seemed wrong, even dangerous, to eat the cakes. Nyxie had fussed and fumed. But she knew that Thea wouldn't budge. And so still the cakes remained untouched.

Until now.

Thea went to the hearth and stirred the coals with a stick. The red glow pushed back the shadows for a moment. She took up one of the cakes, broke it, and sniffed. It smelled good, very good. Nuts and maple sugar, poppy seeds and nice wheat flour, not the coarse corn and oats they had to eat most times.

Expecting it to smolder and smoke, she broke a small piece off the cake and tossed it into the coals. Instead it burst suddenly into a brilliant greenish flame. She threw the rest of the cake into the fire. And for a moment, the light was strong enough to read by.

She stared in wonderment at the thrashing, spitting flames.

There were five cakes left. She threw them all in together, and the sudden burst of flame pushed all the shadows out of the room.

The heat was strong enough to drive her back. And when the flames died down, her sight was blurred with bright flickers.

She wasn't so much afraid now as confused. Why? What might have been in the cakes? What did the old woman really want from her? She was sure now that Roddy hadn't been the real object of her visit. Fecula wanted to see her, wanted to hold her hand and look into her eyes.

Thea watched till the flames were gone completely, then went to her father's room.

He was half asleep, murmuring and moving his hands as though drawing an invisible map. One candle burned by the bedside, weak and low.

Thea sat down by her father and took his hand. He stirred

a little, turning to look her way. But his mind was still cloudy and muddled.

It had been a long hard day. She wanted sleep more than anything. But she also wanted to stay by her father's side. So she leaned in and nestled her head against the pillow. She wanted comfort from him, his arm around her shoulder, soothing words. Instead, she was the nurse and the protector. King Ivars's breath came in soft whistles. The candle burned lower and lower. Sleep covered Thea, as a rising tide covers a beach.

3 5

Thea woke, sensing another person breathing nearby. She didn't hear it. She *felt* it — a soft, steady in and out of black night air.

"Who —" she whispered. The candle was out, yet a pulsing yellow light bathed her, the bed, and her father's beard and wild mane of white hair.

Then she saw Scalander looming near. His eyes were fixed on her, like two lanterns casting two beams of soft, gold light. "Pretty, pretty, pretty," he hissed.

Thea didn't scream, though she felt the loud cry boiling in her as steam builds in a kettle. She didn't run. Nor stand between him and her father. She didn't ask who he was.

She just sat there, dreamy and weak. He was doom. She knew that. His presence there meant nothing but wrongness and suffering and traveling down a dark, dreadful path. Still, she sat quietly, waiting for him to speak.

"Mother," he hissed, almost too quiet to hear, "has lain the bad hand on him." He spoke so slowly, it seemed time itself was running down.

"Why? Why would she do such a thing?" Thea responded. Sickness, a curse — the old woman had concocted something terrible that would take her father to the grave. "Papa never hurt her. He never did anyone any harm."

"Persuasion," Scalander said, stretching the word out impossibly long.

Thea rose unsteadily. "What do you mean? What do you want?" Her voice was rising. Still, Ivars slept on. She knew that he wouldn't wake till Scalander wanted him to. And the others too. The whole house was under his baleful influence. Sleep, heavy clouds of sleep, filled the rooms. She could scream "fire" and "murder" and no one would come to help.

"What do you want?"

"Only you. Only the pretty thing. Only Scalander's queen." He came closer, as a shadow would move. "We've waited and waited a long time. Mother promised a royal girl. And here you are. Scalander's queen forever."

A vast weight seemed to press on Thea. The thousand pounds of guilt she felt for driving Roddy away was like doves' feathers compared to this. "That can't be. I'm just a girl. This can't be happening. I'm too young."

"No, so pretty. Scalander's princess."

His fist opened, and inside was a golden ring. It too shed its own light, though softer and cooler than his eyes. "Persuasion. We make a bargain."

He held the ring out. Thea crossed her arms and buried her hands. She shook her head fiercely. "It cannot be. Never."

"Mother has lain the bad hand on him." Scalander nodded toward the bed. His speech came easier now. The words were like old tools, needing to be brought out and used. "The old man will not rise. He will not open his eyes. Till you are Scalander's queen."

Now the weight crushed all the air from Thea's lungs. It pressed her back into the chair, where she clung like a survivor in a shipwreck.

"The crows have gathered, all my black legions. They've decided as one. Every scream you hear from the sky is a yes." The ring lay in his palm. "Take it for a cure. You wear the ring as Scalander's queen and the old man will live."

"I'm just a girl. I'm just —"

"The crows have said yes. And Mother has said yes. And now is Scalander's turn: Yes!" His eyes glowed brighter. "Yes, yes."

Thea hunched in on herself, squeezing her arms against her chest. She shut her eyes and turned away. But still she could see the beautiful golden ring glowing like a circle of captured sunlight. "I cannot. I will not. Never."

"Then your dear old father will never rise from his bed."

"Go away! Go away!" Thea groaned.

"When you're ready, take the path into the Bastery Wood."

After a long silence, Thea opened one eye. Scalander was gone. But the ring lay on her father's bed. It cast only a faint glow now. And as she watched, even that faded to nothing.

36

As Scalander had warned, the next day the old king did not open his eyes. He lay there, still feverish, still lost in dreamland. Thea soaked cloths and wiped his sweaty brow. She held his hand and thought she saw some change in his face when she talked. "Papa. Papa, it's me. Your Thea is here."

Nyxie sat at the foot of the bed, sniffling.

Mina was working in the kitchen, trying to pretend that everything was as it should be. She even tried to whistle a glad song, though Thea heard it crack and waver.

"What if he doesn't wake up?" Nyxie whispered. "What'll we do? We can't get along all by ourselves."

"Don't fret so," Thea said. "He'll be better soon. This will pass, and he'll be fine again." She didn't believe it, though. She knew that the old woman's curse would last forever unless she went to the Bastery Wood to be Scalander's bride.

She had the ring in her apron pocket. She slipped her hand out of her father's and held the little circle of warm gold. All I've got to do, she thought, is put it on, and Papa will be fine and healthy again.

Is that too much to ask of a daughter? she wondered. Yes, it would be a terrible sacrifice. But her papa would do the same to save her, wouldn't he? He'd give up something precious. He'd go away and never come back, if it meant saving one of his daughters' lives.

He was muttering now, words in Latin and German and a few in English. It was nonsense, as crazy as the dreams Thea knew he must be having. She turned her head away, so that Nyxie couldn't see her tears. Her finger toyed with the ring. Warm, always warm. Even if she sunk the ring in the cool springhouse stream, she knew it would warm itself in a moment.

"You'll be fine, Papa," she murmured. "Everything's going to be just fine."

"Do you think so?" Nyxie asked, wiping her nose on her sleeve. "Do you think he'll get better?"

"Of course." But Thea was thinking of her mother, and

how she'd laid down and never gotten up again. "Of course he'll get better. In a few days, he'll be up and around just like before."

Nyxie tried to smile, crooked and weak. Thea tried too. Then she turned back to her father, wiping his forehead with a damp cloth.

37

Roddy did a few chores around the farm, cutting wood and digging up the old kitchen garden. He put all his muscle into the work, as he had put all of himself into turning Mr. Queed's crank. Work can take your mind off your suffering. That's what his mother used to say. Work can push back all the fears and troubles and the voices we should never listen to.

Roddy stabbed his shovel into the ground. He pressed with one foot on the shovel and turned over a big clump of weedy earth. Again and again, digging till his shoulders ached and blisters rose on his palms.

But still he heard sounds that might turn into voices if he listened close enough. The crows were gone, with their crazy chatter. Yet the sky and the land, the tiny creatures of the field and the movement of the wind, all whispered to him.

A bright, hot stinging cut through his hand. He put aside

the shovel for a moment and looked at his palms. One of the blisters had opened, and a trickle of clear ooze ran down.

"Enough, enough, enough!" he moaned. He could work till the sun went down, and still his feelings would be there inside him. Pain didn't drive them away, nor hard labor. The hurt that filled his heart was greater, not less, than it had been that morning.

There was the old question that gnawed him like a dog gnaws a bone. Why had he been sent away by his parents? Why was he the one cast off by the family?

But a new suffering had risen up too. The old man had chosen him, and now he was lying sick in bed. The girls, he'd thought, might be his friends. Yet they blamed him for Ivars's sickness. They thought of him as the sailors in the Bible thought of Jonah. He carried a curse. And as long as he was with them, bad things would press them on every side.

He could go back to the ropeworks. There was always employment there. It was awful, dismal, empty labor. But at least there he knew who he was and what he must do. Round and round and round with the creaking wooden crank.

Roddy spat on his hand, wiped the mud away as best he

could, and set off for Pharaoh. Mr. Queed will take me back, he thought. He has his bag of silver. And he can have his rope-monkey too.

He trudged along the path, like a lost soldier trying to find his home after the battle is over. But there was no home. His mother and father had sold him away. Mr. Queed had sold him too. King Ivars was too sick to help. And Thea surely didn't want him around.

He reached the road and stopped. One way pointed toward Pharaoh. The other led westward, to places Roddy had never been. If he had a penny, he'd flip it to decide his direction. Instead, he saw a little chokecherry bush and plucked a sprig of last year's fruit. They were tiny and puckered, and hard to pull off. But like playing the "she loves me, she loves me not" game with a daisy, he removed the fruit one at a time. "West, east, west, east," he murmured.

He came to the last of the withered cherries, and headed west, toward an unknown place.

38

Thea sat with her father after supper. The shadows deepened. They drew nearer. Thea lit another candle and adjusted the silver reflector behind to cast more light. Still, the darkness came on as a tide rises.

King Ivars looked worse now. His cheeks were sunken and blackness circled his eyes. His breathing came weaker than before. He'd eaten nothing for two days. And the only water he'd taken was that which the girls trickled into his mouth from a wet cloth.

If this goes on much longer, Thea thought, he'll shrink down to bones and wrinkles.

"Papa," Thea whispered. "I'm going to fetch a doctor in town." He must have heard, for he groaned a little. "It's for the best. We don't have any medicine. We don't know what's wrong or how to make you better." She was holding his hand, squeezing. "Papa, I know it'll make you angry. But we can't lose you. We can't get along here, just three girls, without you."

He trembled. His hands clutched at the air. A whistling noise came from his mouth. But no words.

"You watch him now," Thea said to her little sister. "Try to get him to drink a little water."

She kissed her father on his old withered forehead, thinking, This might be the last time, and left.

39

All the way to town, she felt something or someone following her. Dusk was well along as she hurried down the path. Again and again, she stopped, listening. But the woods were quiet. No wagons or mules were out that evening. No young men were heading to see their sweethearts. No travelers were approaching Pharaoh.

Coming out of the woods, Thea stopped and turned quickly. Yes, there behind her were rustling and faint footsteps. "What do you want?" she called out. "Why are you following me?"

Her hand groped in her apron pocket, finding the ring which Scalander had left. It was warm, smooth, a perfect circle which she knew would fit her finger exactly.

"Why?" she shouted into the shadows. "Why me?" There was anger in her voice, and tears too. She was scared, more scared than she'd ever been. Her father was sick, perhaps never to wake. Her mother was gone forever. And now a pair of foul yellow eyes followed her everywhere.

She held the gold ring as though to toss it away. "I will! I swear I will," she shouted.

The rustling came again, and the leaves parted. A black dog emerged, staring at her with eyes she'd seen before.

If he talks, Thea thought, I won't be able to stand it. Already weak, she knew one more strange happening would make her fall apart right then and there. "This place is terrible," she said aloud. "Too many charms. Bad charms, good charms, it's all the same."

She closed her eyes, wishing as hard as she could that she were home again. Not the old Seven place, but the castle in Schatzburg. Not alone with her sick old father, but surrounded by servants, by a thousand candles pushing away the darkness. She wanted her mother to hold her hand and say, "Everything will be just fine."

The dog came closer. Thea heard the scratch of its paws in the dirt. She opened her eyes and faced him, a thin, sleek creature that somehow seemed to slither, though it walked on four legs.

If it barked or snarled, she would have been less afraid. But the beast just stared at her with those eyes that cast their own faint light. It circled round her and she turned, to follow its course.

Round and round they went, and Thea thought of an old witch-man who'd come to the castle once to show her father some so-called spells. He'd walked in circles, muttering. He'd waved a willow wand and nodded. But nothing had happened. It was all foolishness, a trick. King Ivars had sent the man away, warning him to never try such a thing again.

Now, however, on this moonlit road, Thea thought that a real spell might be cast by the dog's endless circling.

"You promise?" she said at last to the black dog. "You give me your solemn promise that my papa will wake up if I put on your ring?"

The dog stopped. It glared silently at her.

"The curse will be off him forever? You promise me that?" She was crying now, but not sobs and big tears. She was crying mostly on the inside. Her eyes were misted over, and a heat filled her face. Her chest felt all weak and trembly. "You give me your promise? No more curse? You'll take it away? Papa will wake up and be fine again?"

The dog gave one slow nod.

40

Roddy passed at first through woodlands, with a few scrubby fields scattered here and there. He saw only one cabin, abandoned, he guessed, for years. The door was missing, and the chimney was falling apart.

Then the woods got denser and edged closer to the road. Roddy walked and the hours passed. Darkness came on, slow and steady, as though Roddy were walking directly from a daylight world into the land of night.

Hunger grew in his belly. His feet hurt from traveling so long. Cold dampness rose from the forest floor.

The moon rose. It seemed to tremble, and a gust of black wind came up from nowhere. A tremor went through Roddy, as when you feel someone's eyes are on you but know you are alone. Then a black figure was before him, astride a sorry skeleton of a horse.

"Boy," the rider said in a voice like a wheezing reed organ. "Boy! You live hereabouts?"

Roddy didn't answer. For if truth be told he was still unsure if this apparition was ghost or man. And to speak with a spirit, he feared, might give it more power, a firmer toehold in our world.

"Boy. Where is your home?"

Roddy almost said, "I have no home." However, he stayed silent.

The rider wore a great flopping hat, which cast a shadow over his face. But as he came through darkness and into a swath of moonlight, Roddy got a clear look at him. His eyes were wild and bright. His gaunt face seemed full of pain, or perhaps some desire Roddy did not understand. "Can you speak, or has a spirit of dumbness taken hold of your heart?"

His look sent a cold dart of fear into Roddy's breast. Yet he had one advantage over the stranger. For then he knew who the man was. He'd heard stories the last few months of the great fierce preacher named Lorenzo Dow. Mr. Queed, like many others, had called him Crazy Dow. His ways were strange, his words too hard for many ears, his face terrible to behold.

He rode the night winds, a scarecrow on horseback. The sound he made as he went was like dead leaves rustling on a tree. He was thin, tall, and dressed all in black.

"Answer me, boy."

Roddy's tongue remained still. The preacher might have been famous from Maine to Alabama. His sermons may have melted congregations to sobs and flowing tears. It was even said that at his command demons would flee. And some folks believed Reverend Dow could bring back a sufferer from the very doorstep of death. Yet he could not make Roddy speak if he chose to remain dumb.

They faced each other there in the moon-spangled dark.

Roddy heard Mr. Queed's voice, from a few weeks back. "A bird of ill omen," Mr. Queed had called the preacher. "Ragged in his black cloak. Here today and then gone on the morrow. He talks of the love of God, but he carries salvation in both hands like an ax."

Preacher Dow dug his heels into the old nag's sides. The horse took a few steps closer. "Where are you headed, boy?"

Roddy couldn't have answered that, even if he wanted to.

"You can hear. That's plain," he said. "And I'd wager, if I

were a wagering man, that your speech is good too." The preacher edged his horse nearer.

"Which way are you going?" Roddy whispered.

"Where the Lord directs," the Reverend Dow declared. "Where I am needed. Where I might serve best and fight to save a precious soul."

"How do you know where you're needed? How can you be sure?"

"The heart is my compass. North, south, east, west. It knows the true path." The preacher came closer yet. Roddy could see a fire in the man's eyes, something like madness. Yet there was truth in what he said. "You can flee all your life, and still what you flee will be there dead straight ahead. What are you running from, boy?

"Nothing," Roddy said. "And everything."

"No matter which way you run, it'll be there right in front of you. You hark my words, now, boy. If you must run, go toward something, not away."

And with that, the preacher was gone. Shadows closed around him as curtains close around an actor on the stage. Darkness fell, and silence too, complete and deep as a well.

41

"Where are you going?" Mr. Queed asked. "At this hour, what errand calls you out?"

Old Mother Fecula was tying on her bonnet, making two big bows with the black ribbons. She picked up her basket and nodded a goodbye to Mr. Queed.

"A wedding! A wedding," she sang, in a voice like a creaking shutter. "Tonight my precious boy takes his bride."

"Tonight?" Mr. Queed said, looking out the kitchen window. It was nearly midnight. The town of Pharaoh lay quiet as a cave. Most nights Mr. Queed was in bed at this time. But bad dreams had woken him, sent him wandering around the house.

"I'm off to celebrate with my boy," Fecula said. "For his chosen one has said yes, yes, yes."

Mr. Queed was holding a candle. His nightshirt hung to

the floor. He hadn't put in his false teeth, so his mouth gaped like an empty purse.

The old woman pinched her own cheeks to bring out a little color. Then she took from her apron pocket a little man made of wax. He had a crown made of silver thread and a beard of white wool. "One more task and I can set out on my happy journey."

Fecula knelt by the fire, blowing on the coals. When they'd risen to a cheery orange glow, she whistled a few quavering notes and tossed the wax man in.

"Little toy king," she chanted, "now be well, you are free, here ends my spell."

He melted quickly, head and arms softening to liquid. Then he burst into flame and was quickly gone. Mother Fecula murmured, "Done. The curse is burned away, and the happy day can begin."

42

King Ivars's fever broke that night. And by morning his thoughts were clear as they'd ever been. At dawn, he sat up in bed, calling for his girls. Mina came in first, thrilled to see him so much better. Then Nyxie joined them, flopping down on the bed and hugging her father around the neck.

"Where's Thea?" the old man asked.

The girls were silent.

"What's wrong with her? She doesn't have the fever now, does she?"

"No, Papa. She's not ill."

"Then where is she?" He swung his feet to the floor. "Thea!" he called. "Thea, your old papa is feeling all himself again!"

"She's gone," Mina said. "She didn't come back last night."

"What do you mean? Where did she go?"

"She said she was going into town to fetch the doctorman. But she never came back."

King Ivars tried to stand, but fell back to the bed. Mina

held on to him, saying quietly, "You should get more sleep, Papa. The fever broke, but you're not all the way better."

He tried again to stand. "We've got to find her. Something's wrong. Terribly wrong. She's never stayed out —"

"I'll go and look for her," Mina said. "Nyxie can stay here, now that you're better."

Mina got her shawl and bonnet, but before she could leave, the door opened. In came Roddy, smelling of mule and long travel.

"Thea's gone!" Nyxie cried. "Did you see her?"

Roddy collapsed into a chair. "Get him something to eat," Ivars told his girls. Mina was back in a minute with a piece of yesterday's bread smeared with honey.

"I saw Fecula, the old woman," Roddy whispered. "She was going toward the Bastery Wood. She said she was going to a wedding. I thought this was nonsense. She pointed at me and said something about 'the pretty one with the soft brown eyes.' Sometimes she acts like a lunatic, not making a bit of sense. But this time —"

Mina translated, and King Ivars hung his head, moaning softly. "I remember now. I was asleep. Or I was in the black pit of the fever. Thea was here. She was talking to me. She didn't know if I could hear, but she kept talking." He tried to stand again. Mina helped him stay on his feet. He took a deep breath and stood up as straight as he could.

"We've got to find her," Ivars said. "She's gone off to the woods. It was to save me, to break the fever."

"Don't be foolish, Papa. You need to lie back down."

But Ivars shook Mina's hands off him. "It was a bargain: Thea's hand in marriage for the words that would cure my fever."

"Papa, you're still weak. Maybe when you've rested some more —"

"We go now," the old man said in English. "Can you come, boy?"

Roddy gulped down the rest of the bread. And wiping his hands on his pant legs, he stood up.

"We go," Ivars said, tottering toward the door.

"Papa, this is madness! Get back in that bed."

But he was, after all, a king, not just a weak old man. Roddy went with him outside. There was Lottie, one of Mr. Queed's mules. "I snuck by the ropeworks last night and got her. I was so tired, I think I fell asleep riding her back here."

He helped the old king onto Lottie's back, and they set off to find Thea.

43

Though it was morning, a heavy weight of darkness pressed in on Thea. The path was clear and well trodden. It led inward, directly to the heart of the Bastery Wood.

No woodsman's ax had touched these oaks and beech trees. They rose up like the pillars of some vast cathedral. They're so big, they might hold up the sky, Thea thought. Thin spears of yellow morning light stabbed down from the leafy vault above.

As Thea moved deeper into the woods, where slender black creeks cut through the landscape, tangled vines and brush crowded the pathway.

She held Scalander's golden ring as a compass. But she had not yet slipped it onto her finger. To give up and head into the woods was one thing. She could abandon hope for her own happiness to save her father. However, to put the ring on, to promise for all time to be Scalander's, this she could not yet do.

Where is he? she wondered. Would she have to walk for

days in the woods to find him? Or would he skulk along in the shadows, watching and waiting for the right moment to reveal himself?

Was there a palace waiting for her? Or a dismal forest shack? Perhaps his house was built in the treetops, she thought. Or might he have an underground burrow like the snakes and badgers and foxes?

In a few years, I'll be just a memory. They'll talk about me the way people recall a stranger who'd once passed through town. There was another one, people will say. Didn't the old man have a third daughter? The middle child is always the one they forget. The oldest is the pride and joy. The youngest, the baby, is the one whom everyone dotes on. But the middle girl, she can be sacrificed, given up, lost.

Thea heard the flutter of wings above. There on the branch of a sugar maple was one lone crow.

He watched her with glistening yellow eyes. As she passed underneath, he gave up one loud, glad cry and flew away. The noise echoed a long time, longer, it seemed to Thea, than was natural.

44

King Ivars rode the mule, and Roddy walked alongside.

They were soon inside the woods, traveling the same path Thea had gone along only a few hours before. Beetles and bees made a soft brittle hum. The trees leaned together as though whispering to each other. Far above, Roddy could hear the wind moving. But where they went, along the narrow pathway, the air was still.

"The old woman," Ivars said. "She came. Out to us. To the house." He struggled with the English words, but Roddy understood enough.

Mother Fecula had gone this way too. He knew that now. Not by smell or sight of footprints. Some other sense told him of her passing. It was as when a boat travels through still waters. It seemed he could see little ripples and eddies in the air where she'd been.

Ivars muttered in a half dozen strange languages. Perhaps

he's praying, Roddy thought. Or casting a spell of his own. Taking a good look at the old man, though, Roddy thought the jumbled words were more likely just the nonsense of a man recently woken from a long fever.

He took hold of Lottie's traces as they came down a rocky slope. At the bottom he felt again the air was disturbed, as though he were looking through a blurry window. "Mother Fecula's been here," he said.

King Ivars perked up a little, stroked his beard, and nodded.

"Not that long ago. Don't worry. We'll find Thea before she does."

The king jabbed his heels into Lottie's sides to get her moving a little faster. "Another," Ivars said. "She's going to see another one. The king." He paused, looking for the right words. "The King of Shadows."

Hearing this, Roddy tugged harder on Lottie's traces. They hurried as best they could along the trail, moving into deeper, heavier, longer shadows.

45

Simeon Queed pounded the handle of his whip on the front door. Behind him, in the wagon, were all his rope-monkeys. They'd come to help carry away Ivars's treasure. Whole kegs full of gold, buckets and barrels and chests and boxes. Enough diamonds and emeralds to make a dozen crowns. That's what Mr. Queed had told the boys they'd find that day. They all came gladly. Anything was better than slaving at the rope-works. But traveling out to the old Seven house, and seeing, let alone seizing, a king's fortune—this only happened once in a lifetime.

Mr. Queed pounded louder. Getting no response, he threw the door back. There were two of the girls, cowering by the fire. The older one held a flintlock pistol. She pointed it at Mr. Queed. But her hand was shaking so much he doubted she could even pull the trigger.

"Go away," Mina whispered. "Now. I command it. Go away from this place."

Sneering, Mr. Queed strode into the room. "Put that down, princess. You're going to hurt yourself."

In the doorway behind, Frank Beasling appeared, sniffing the air like a cowardly cur-dog.

"Give it here," Mr. Queed said, reaching toward her. Mina grasped the flintlock with both hands and squeezed the trigger. The hammer fell with a hollow click. No crack of fire. No puff of smoke. No lead ball exploding from the barrel.

Mina tried to yank the hammer back. But Mr. Queed took hold of the pistol and jerked it out of her grasp. "No more such nonsense," he growled. "Tell us where you have the gold hidden, and we'll soon be gone."

"Go away," Nyxie whispered. "We didn't do you any harm."

Frank came into the room and said too loudly, "You mind your mouth around Mr. Queed. You show him the proper respect and we won't have to hurt anybody."

Mr. Queed put the flintlock down carefully on the kitchen table, then sat in a chair to face the two girls. "Your father and the boy are gone. And the middle sister too. There's no one now to protect the pretty ones." He took Mina by the chin and turned her face to the firelight. "They say in town you really are princesses. I do believe this isn't a lie. You surely don't have the look of our homespun girls."

Mina slapped his hand away, screaming, "How dare you touch me!"

Mr. Queed sneered back at her. "You might be royalty in the old country. But we don't care much about such things in America. Here you're just pretty girls who have to do as you're told. No such thing as princesses here."

"There isn't any gold," Mina said.

Mr. Queed slapped her hard, just once, on the cheek. Mina screamed and swore and tried to slap him back. She'd never been hit in her entire life. And except for her nurse, when she was a baby, she'd never even been touched by a commoner.

Raging, she lunged at him, but Frank Beasling grabbed her by the wrists and pulled her arms around behind her back.

"Tell me, right now, where the gold is."

"She's told you the truth," Nyxie said. "There isn't any gold. It's all silver."

Mr. Queed smiled. "Then kindly show me to your silver and we'll soon be on our way."

"Nyxie! Don't you say a word!" Mina shouted.

At a nod from Mr. Queed, Frank pulled her by the wrists out of the room.

"Now, be a good girl and tell us."

Mina screamed and cried. Frank dragged her out to the wagon and soon had her hands tied to the big wooden wheel. The other boys all stared at such a thing. Their first sight of a princess, and she was tied up like a common slave.

Inside the Seven house, Mr. Queed was smiling his black smile and wheedling with Nyxie. "Just tell me where it is and we'll be gone. No harm done. No hard feelings. Here in America we don't have royalty. So it's not right that your father should have all that treasure. This is a democracy. We all get to be rich here."

He petted her hair with one hand and held her chin with the other, squeezing tightly. "You be a good girl now," he whispered. "Do as you're told and everything will be fine. We'll bring your father and your sister home, and everything will be just fine."

At last Nyxie broke down and told where the treasure was hidden: "Down at the springhouse. Papa put all the silver in some old kegs. It's down there keeping cool. Papa wanted the money there. He said it was bad too close to the fire."

Mr. Queed bolted from the house. "Come on!" he shouted. "All of you!" He led them down a short path to the spring-house. Nyxie had told the truth. There were two wooden casks such as whiskey or cider was stored in. And inside, as Nyxie had said, were thousands of silver coins.

Mr. Queed grabbed two handfuls and held them to his mouth, as though kissing the silver.

"Grab hold!" he commanded after a moment. "Go on, all of you put your backs to it." He replaced the lids. The rope-monkeys tipped the casks on their sides and got to work rolling them back to the wagon.

Mr. Queed led the way, like a priest at the head of some strange procession.

Reaching the wagon, he quickly untied Mina and told her she was free to go. She just stood there as the boys rolled the kegs up boards into the back of the wagon. Nyxie came out, and they both stood weeping as Mr. Queed cracked his whip on the mule's back. "You boys walk back," he said. "Too much weight for you to ride."

He turned the wagon and set off, singing and whistling and smiling in the warm sunlight.

46

Was it dusk already? Thea asked herself. She hadn't seen the sun for hours. This deep in the Bastery Wood, under the dark leafy roof, the sun was always hidden. Something was different now, however. The shadows were not like before. They weren't just dark, but had a purplish shimmer.

Mostly the ground was covered with a hundred years of dead leaves. Here and there though, a great glittering spike of stone jutted up from the forest floor. Like icebergs in the darkling night sea, these rocks seemed lonesome and cold and ancient.

Thea thought of her sisters then, and her father too. She hoped, she trusted, that now the fever-spell was gone. Likely, now her father was up and pottering around the house. Mina and Nyxie were probably just then getting ready for bed, telling stories of the old country or singing a song together.

"They don't miss me," she whispered. They don't need me.

Mina can cook and make sure Papa takes care of himself. Nyxie can sing and prattle and bring a little sunshine into Papa's heart. Mina will marry a rich young man soon enough. And then they'll all be taken care of. In a month or two I'll just be a memory. And in a few years, not even that. It'll be fine. I'll do my duty and everything will be as it should be. That's what she thought as she hiked along the winding path. But what she felt was surely different.

This place was getting stranger with every footstep she took. Darker, yes. But somehow brighter too, like clouds when the moon is behind them. All the shapes she saw now wavered and swayed. Huge old oaks and sycamores seemed to be made of black vapor. The glittering boulders came near, then appeared to retreat.

Was it night? Probably. Did the moon shine somewhere above the black forest vault? Most likely.

But where Thea walked it was always this way.

And she knew, by these signs, that soon Scalander would appear. This was his place, his kingdom, his world. These were the outer reaches of his Court of Shadows.

Thea closed her hand on the golden ring he'd given to her. Would it be so bad? she asked herself. I'll be queen here.

Queen of Shadows. No papa and no sisters. But I will rule here and wear a crown. No more the second sister but the one and only. He wanted me, she thought. He picked me of all three girls. He saw what no one else had seen.

A day or two before, these thoughts would have seemed monstrous to Thea. How could she consider marrying Scalander to be anything but dreadful?

Here though, in this beautiful dim nowhere, her feelings had shifted.

And her thoughts went with them. Since she was little, she'd thought of what it would be like on her wedding day. The bells ringing in St. Gottfried's tower, a long white dress, a choir of children, and her parents smiling their approval.

Thea held the ring tight in her fist. She squeezed till her hand hurt, then squeezed even tighter.

She was thousands of miles from home. Her mother was gone, and her father was lost to her. She'd never see the beautiful cathedral again, nor hear the bells pealing. No white silk dress, but plain homespun. No choirs of angelic children, but only flocks of screaming crows.

There, up ahead, she saw a broad shaft of pale white light. A break in the trees allowed the sky's dim shine into the forest. And in this circle of soft glow was a black figure. He stood with his hands on his hips and his shoulders thrown back. His eyes were bright, burning like two little lanterns.

"We meet by moonlight, proud Thea." His voice echoed in the gloomy spaces around her. "But not so proud anymore."

She went toward him, feeling her insides turn weak as water.

47

Old Mother Fecula hobbled as fast as she could through the forest. With her cane, like a three-legged beast, she went up and down, around and through, hurrying as best she might to be with her darling boy on this night of nights.

Happiness grew in her as storm clouds gather in the sky. Full of lightning soon to strike. Full of thunder soon to rumble across the landscape. Full of hard, cold, bitter rain.

"What we want," she chanted as she walked. "What we want, we shall have."

With every step, she stabbed her cane into the soft, leafy ground.

"What we want shall soon be ours. The sweetest bloom of the sweetest flowers."

Left, right, stab the cane. Left, right, and down again.

"What my boy needs shall now be his. We've waited long and now it is."

Her breath puffed and wheezed like a steam engine with too much fire in the boiler.

"We have our prize, we stake our claim, we say aloud our joy's sweet name."

48

"Thea, welcome. Welcome to your new home." Scalander bowed low and swept his arm through the air.

The moon shone as a great lantern. She thought he might pluck it down from the sky and hand it to her as a king could give a little glittering bauble to a child.

"You've made your choice," he said. "And it is good."

Walking through the woods had been like a dream. And so, meeting Scalander in this beam of moonlight should have been like waking. But Thea felt herself even more lost, more trapped in dreamy confusion.

"Is my papa going to be better? Did she, the old woman, did she take the curse off him?"

"You're here, Thea. And so, he must be risen from his fever bed. A bargain is a bargain. And a promise is a promise." Scalander stood taller than she remembered. His skin was darker, shiny like polished leather. The little ring of spikes on the top of his head seemed more like a crown than before.

Vines hung down from above, thick around as her arm. And night-blooming flowers opened themselves around his feet, wafting out their venom-sweet perfume.

Here was the worst thing she could imagine. Here was a dark forest lord who'd stolen her from her family, from all she knew. And yet part of her felt at ease, even happy. He was terrible and he inspired her with awe. He was grave and graceful, black as a December midnight and beautiful as heaven. She found herself pulled toward him. And at the same time, a small voice whispered for her to run, run as fast as she could away from him.

"My midnight bride," he said, as though announcing her presence to a hall full of guests.

At his feet a spring started bubbling. Was it bright underground water, or perhaps black moonlight somehow pouring from the earth?

Thea felt now that her father's fever had come to her, filled her with strange visions. I'll wake up soon, she told herself. I'll wake up in my bed, and this will all be gone. Mina and Nyxie will be there, and Papa, and he'll smooth back my hair and tell me it was all a bad dream.

"My long-awaited queen," Scalander said.

From the shadows came a black stag, with a great rack of horns and smoldering yellow eyes. He watched from his dim place on the edge of the clearing.

Thea heard the flutter of wings and there was a crow, come to observe this moment also.

Something skittered in the leaves at her feet. And she knew it was the little black newt.

Off in the distance a dog gave out a long, lonesome howl.

Something rustled and chittered in a nearby tree. Thea turned and saw a fat black porcupine drawn up in a spiky ball.

"My kingdom," Scalander said, waving his arm grandly. "And my subjects." The forest creatures came a bit closer, all of them intently watching, quiet now as gravestones.

49

Roddy tugged on the mule's traces, urging her along. King Ivars held on to Lottie's mane with one hand. In the other he carried a pine-knot torch.

They were close now. Roddy could feel it. The old woman must have been here only a few minutes before. Even with the smoke from the torch, Roddy was sure he smelled something sour and strange in the night air. Like the perfume from an ancient flower, sweet and sickening at the same time, Mother Fecula left a trail through the forest.

"Thea will be fine. Don't worry," Roddy kept saying. But he wasn't sure. And King Ivars looked more distressed, more anxious for his daughter's safety, as they strove deeper into the nightwood blackness.

"We'll get there in time," Roddy said. "Nothing bad is going to happen to her." He was speaking English to the old king. It didn't matter what language though. He was talking just to make a sound, to fill up the silence that Ivars had fallen into.

"No one will hurt her." But how would they deliver her from evil? Surely, what Thea needed was a company of strong men. Not an old king barely able to keep steady on a mule's back or a boy whose only skill was turning a crank. What kind of rescuers were they? They had no guns or swords. No Bible or prayers to drive away such evil. Not a knife or fighting stick between them. Not even a religious song that might wound unholy ears.

Still, Roddy kept saying that Thea would be safe. "Soon, very soon," he said. "We'll find her. We'll keep her safe."

He heard a dog give out one long howl. Roddy had never heard such a lonely sound. And coming from the depths of the forest, it added to his feeling of dread.

"We're coming," he said, as though Thea might hear this sad whisper. "We're moving as fast as we can."

50

Mother Fecula arrived at her son's Court of Shadows just as the girl went forward to take Scalander's hand.

Fecula had never seen anything so beautiful. Her son finally was getting all that was due him. He was royal, not just a creature skulking in the woods. That's what she had told him since he was little. "You're a noble, my darling boy, not a forest freak. You're a king, not a monster."

There was music. A swarm of bees buzzed and the trees swayed and creaked in time. Scalander had his scepter, a long white bone. His servants and subjects were gathered to witness the wedding. A red carpet surrounded her son's throne. It was not silk from Persia, but low-creeping plants with tiny scarlet flowers. And there *was* a throne. Scalander sat on a huge stump covered entirely with night-glowing moss. It throbbed with a greenish witch-light, making his proud form seem even more regal.

In one hand he had the scepter. In the other was a circlet of braided vines. No gold and diamonds for Scalander's queen. Just a simple ring of dark tendrils.

"We are ready," Scalander said, as his mother emerged into the clearing.

Thea turned and looked toward the old woman. Fecula was pleased. The girl was bedraggled from her walk through the woods. She was wearing no bridal satins. And yet she was as charming to the eyes as the full moon's glow.

"We've waited long," Fecula said. "But this sight is worth the wait." She hobbled toward the throne, poking with her cane into the soft carpet of tiny flowers.

The girl didn't shrink back as Fecula approached. She stood straight and calm, like a holy martyr going to her terrible fate. Her eyes were open, but what did they see? Though she might bow her head to accept Scalander's crown of vines, what did she feel?

The old woman took her hand, and felt the cool smooth skin quiver at her touch. Was this disgust the girl felt? Or excitement? Was it fever or night chills? She peered into the pretty brown eyes and could see nothing past the shiny surface.

51

Thea's heart went numb as the old woman took her hand. The fear was gone. She'd left that behind on her walk into the forest. Loathing no longer had a place in her breast. Beauty and raw ugliness, these mixed and merged here in the Court of Shadows. Dread and longing too would be impossible to separate now. Like black paint and white all stirred up together, Thea's feelings were a blurry gray.

The old woman truly was awful, grinning and clicking her tongue. Her lips hung loose as she babbled on. A trembling wheeze came with every word she said. In the light of day she would surely be the foulest and ugliest of creatures. Here in shadow, she was even more so. Yet Thea did not shrink from her touch.

She felt her thoughts sliding away, like spilled water seeping into dry sand. Her fear and her yearning both disappeared. Her disgust and her hope drained away. If I'm nothing, she told herself, then nothing can hurt me. If my heart shrivels away then it can't be wounded.

"A true princess," the hag said. "All the way here to America, to this valley, to our forest, just to be your bride and queen."

Scalander had put down his scepter and the crown of vines. He was holding now a huge green leaf in both hands. Like a platter heaped with delights from the royal kitchen, it held all manner of strange forest foods.

"Yes, yes," the old woman cackled. "Sweets for the sweet." She pointed them out one at a time. "Elephant ear mushroom, roasted. Nice strawberries and May apples." These last were tiny white waxy fruits. "Chestnuts cooked with maple sugar. And look here: some tiny garlics. Ah, and he's cut you some sassafras bark and stag's horn lichen too."

She plucked a sprig of peppermint and crushed it between her fingers. "Sweet to the nose and pretty to the eye."

"Eat," Scalander said. One hard and heavy word. "Eat."

Where are my tears? Thea kept asking herself. If only I could cry. Her father used to say that tears could dissolve the hardest iron chains. "Liquid diamonds," he used to call them.

"A girl's tears are stronger than any steel armor." But they did not come.

With numb fingers she picked up a cooked acorn and placed it on her tongue.

"Yes! Yes!" Fecula cooed. "Let the feast begin!"

Thea's tongue tasted nothing, just as her heart felt only dry, gray emptiness.

"Eat!" Scalander said. But just then a noise came from outside the little clearing. The rustle and clomp of a mule walking along a forest path.

"Thea!" came a voice thin as steam. "Thea!" It was her father. He'd come for her. He'd risen from the fever bed and come to take her home.

Scalander put aside the leafy platter and took up his scepter again. Fecula jabbed her cane like a sword, stabbing toward King Ivars's voice. Both of them peered into the darkness.

Now the sound was quite distinct. He was close. "Thea!" The old quavery voice was more beautiful than any music to Thea's ears.

"Papa! Here I am!" she shouted. The strength of her voice surprised her, and it jolted Scalander like the crack of a whip.

He grabbed Thea in arms ten times stronger than her father's. He dragged her backward, toward the black wall of shadow.

But before they could escape, the old king rode into the clearing on a mule, pushing a wash of light before himself with a torch.

"She's ours now," Fecula growled. "We made our bargain and you can't go back on it. I lifted the fever, and she agreed to be my darling's queen. That's all. Now go away. Go back where you came from."

Now King Ivars was off the mule, unsteady but still approaching.

"I burned the little wax man. That was the bargain. You're free from my black fever. Now go away."

Ivars caught his foot on a root and stumbled forward. Thea tried to get loose to help him. But Scalander held on even tighter. Her father grabbed a little sapling, and held on. Then he took a deep breath, straightened up, and kept on coming.

"Give me back my daughter," he said in German. "She didn't know what she was saying. She's too young to make such a bargain. Too young to know what that means."

"It's done! It's done!" Fecula shrieked. "My boy has his

queen. Now turn around before we have to break you like a little twig."

Thea's burst of joy faded quickly, seeing how feeble her father was. He should be home in bed, not out here playing the hero, the rescuer.

"Papa," Thea whispered. "You go back now." He seemed so weak. How could he stand up against Scalander and the old woman? "You've got Mina and Nyxie. You don't need me anymore. It's better this way." She wanted him to take her away. She wanted that more than anything in the world. Yet she also wanted him safe, unharmed, so he could take care of the others.

"I'll be all right here," she murmured. "Really. It won't be so bad."

Since the day her mother had passed away to the next world, Thea had not seen her father cry. He wasn't sobbing or weeping now. But there were tears. A few tears shining in the torchlight.

"You can't have her," Ivars said. He tried to stand up straight like a real king making a grand speech. "I forbid it! And what I forbid must —"

Fecula cut him off with one loud laugh. "Can you forbid

the leaves from coming out in springtime? Can you forbid the sun from rising tomorrow? Can you forbid the rain from falling? No?" She sneered and waved her hand as if to dismiss him. "Then you cannot forbid my darling boy from having his queen."

Ivars tried a last time. "She's too young. She's just —"

"She's just perfect!" Scalander whispered. "Now go away before we have to break you into a hundred pieces."

Her father held the torch out, like a sword. Scalander hissed and cursed, as the smoky flame slashed through the air. Mother Fecula shouted for him to back away, and came between them, ever protecting her darling boy.

"Go," she raged. "Take your torch away or I'll cook you in a fever that will never end."

But King Ivars had a shred of fight left in him. Seeing that Scalander was afraid of the fire, he tried again to drive him away from Thea.

"You old fool!" Fecula screamed. "You leave my boy alone." She clapped her hands once, twice, three times. Above them suddenly there was a swirling, jabbering cloud of crows. She waved her cane above her head, as though stirring the air, and the crows turned like a whirlpool made of shadow.

"They'll pick your bones clean," Fecula said. "They'll tear every fleck of meat off your carcass."

Thea's mind was collapsing in on itself. The awful old woman, the curses and threats, Scalander holding her like iron chains, her papa tottering under the terrible swarming crows. It was all too much for her to stand.

But another flame was burning now, on the edge of the clearing. And a new voice broke into the awful din. King Ivars fell to the ground, motionless. His torch sputtered a short distance away. Yet this second flame was much brighter. And it seemed to be saying her name.

52

"Thea, it's me! It's Roddy."

He saw the old king lying on the ground, helpless. He saw Mother Fecula waving her hand crazily in the air. He saw Thea, and behind her a murky black cloud.

The old woman snarled like a beast in a trap. "Get away from here! Go back where you came from. You leave my boy alone."

The torchlight seemed an agony to her. She held her hands over her eyes, moaning and shaking.

As Roddy approached Thea, the darkness behind shifted. He could see a pair of yellow eyes there, but not yet a solid form. "Thea, it's me. We came to bring you back."

Was it a black dog he saw? It reared up on its hind legs, or so it seemed. Roddy thrust out the torch and the creature fell to the ground, cringing and hissing. A wild cat? No, now it seemed a snake or lizard. It feared the light. That much was for sure. When he jabbed the torch at it, the creature shrunk away.

"We came to fetch you home," Roddy said, reaching out one hand to Thea.

"Leave him alone!" Mother Fecula shrieked. She was fumbling in her apron pockets, pulling out sticks, little glass bottles, beads and a knife, a wad of wax and a handful of dry leaves. "Leave my darling alone!"

But Roddy kept thrusting with his torch, driving the nebulous creature backward.

The black beast had let go of Thea now. Dazed, she still stood there, unmoving. Roddy heard the flap of wings and far-off cawing.

"Leave him!" Fecula shouted, and lunged at Roddy. Her old withered hands closed around him like two living vines. His torch waved above. Then Fecula grabbed it away, and with a wild grunt of effort, threw it into the brush.

"It's all right now," Fecula called out. And the yellow eyes came closer. The black creature grew more solid and more like a man now. Roddy trembled to see it, both animal and human, lordly and lowly as dirt.

But Thea finally shook off her daze. She went for her father's torch, which sputtered in the weeds. She took it up, and waving it over her head, brought the flame back to life.

Awful noises came from the living shadow as she approached it. Broken words, snarls of pain, a rattling wheeze. Like a knight with an invincible sword, Thea thrust the torch directly into the heart of the beast. It didn't scream in pain, as Roddy had expected. It didn't fight back or try to escape.

With both hands, Thea held the torch in the center of the dark mass.

And steadily, the flame grew fainter, as if the shadow were drinking up the last of the light. The torch wavered and flickered, then died.

The black, manlike form broke apart as a solid mass of smoke would, hit by a sudden wind. At first Roddy thought it was all gone. But no, it was merely shifting to its final shape, dissolving into ten thousand little black specks.

Then the shadow-shape rose as a cloud of flies. It swirled upward, a buzzing spiral, and was gone.

53

Thea heard Roddy talking, asking questions. He was holding her hands, both of them. He was squeezing them and saying, "What was it? What was that black thing?"

Then Thea heard another voice, her father, weak and far-away. He was speaking German, asking if she was safe.

This brought her all the way back. "Yes, Papa, I'm right here."

She ran to where he lay, held him and brushed the leaves off his face. "Everything is going to be fine now," she murmured. "He's gone. They're both gone."

Fecula had fled, seeing her darling swirl away in the form of the swarming flies. With a tortured shriek, she'd vanished into the darkness of the woods.

All was silence now around them. All was still and cool as the bottom of a well.

Roddy knelt down by the old king and held onto him too. And the three of them stayed there, like that, till a little blur of morning light could be seen through the tops of the trees.

Lottie, the mule, had wandered off during the fight. But she returned in time to carry Ivars back the way he'd come. And so Thea and Roddy walked, and the old king rode. They trusted Lottie to find the way home.

The sun was well up by the time they emerged from the Bastery Wood. It seemed to Thea she'd been in the forest shadows for a week. She was hungry and tired and dirty. But worse: the whole way back, every time she closed her eyes, she could see Scalander in her mind. Royal, yes. And even beautiful with those glowing eyes and crown of black spikes. But he was awful too, awful beyond words.

A few times, as they headed home, Roddy asked Thea what it was he'd seen there in the clearing. Ivars told him to hush. "Not now, boy," he whispered. "Leave her be."

So Thea was alone with her thoughts, with her feelings of sick dread. While still in the woods, she heard the flutter of wings, and all the fear rushed back. "Just some sparrows," her father said, and she calmed.

Then she felt a buzzing around her ear, and slapped frantically. It was only a mosquito. Still, she was glad when they reached the place where the trees gave way and the sunshine flooded the land.

Safe again, Thea thought. I'm safe here in the light.

54

Mina and Nyxie ran out to greet them. They'd both been crying. And at seeing their father again, so worn out he could barely sit on the mule's back, the tears started up again.

Both were jabbering at once, overjoyed and overflowing with bad news too. "He came and took the silver," Nyxie kept saying. "The man from town. He came out and made us say where you hid the silver."

"One at a time," Ivars said. "Slower!" Roddy helped him climb down.

Mina said, "The man who runs the rope factory. He came out with all the boys in a wagon. And he tied me to the wheel like I was a common serving girl. Tied me up!"

"It was terrible, Papa," Nyxie chimed in. "He grabbed us both. He said he'd hurt us."

Mina went on. "He took me outside and tied me. And he kept Nyxie in so he could force her to tell. It's all gone, Papa.

Every last silver taler. He rolled the barrels up to the house and put them on his wagon and took them away. We've got nothing left. Nothing at all. We're poor as paupers now."

Ivars led his girls into the house. With his last bit of strength, he made it to his chair by the fireside and flopped down. "We'll get it back," he said. "Don't worry. He can't rob us like that. Soon enough we'll get everything back that belongs to us."

Nyxie and Mina started jabbering again. But this time Thea made them stop. "We need to sleep," she said. "Papa and Roddy and me. We've been going and going all night. We have to sleep now."

At last Mina saw the wisdom of this and took her little sister outside. Roddy headed for his room. Seeing that her father was already snoring in his chair, Thea went to her room and collapsed on her bed like a tree felled by a woodsman's ax.

55

Roddy was the first one up. He tiptoed past the old king and went outside. Both Mina and Nyxie were working as he'd never seen them do before. Sleeves rolled up, hair tied back, they were doing the best they could to cut wood for their supper fire.

It wasn't just Thea who'd been changed overnight. A stranger wandering by would never have believed that Nyxie and Mina had once been princesses. Dirty and draggled, they looked like ordinary farm girls now.

Roddy ran the bucket down into the well. The water was cold, yet it felt good to wash some of the dirt off his face.

It was late afternoon. A perfect stillness had fallen on the farm. Even the knocking of the ax added to the sense of calm. Why couldn't they just go on this way? Roddy wondered. Work and quiet talk. Every day like the one before. Why couldn't they go on like all the other farm families? Plowing, weeding, cutting wood, and drawing water.

But no, it was clear to him. There was one more battle to be fought.

He heard the door squeak open behind him and out came Thea.

"How is Papa?" Mina asked.

"He's going to be fine. I think he'll sleep the rest of the day, all the way till morning. He hardly woke up to walk to his room. "

"Then we ought to get going," Roddy said. They all knew what he meant, though no one had really said it yet.

He found Lottie cropping fresh grass down by the springhouse. "It won't take but an hour to get there," he said. "All the same, we ought to get moving."

It seemed to Roddy he should bring some sort of weapon. But what did he have that could prevail against Mr. Queed? Against the other boys? And worst: against Mother Fecula? Even if he had a shiny cutlass, a good Pennsylvania musket, a whole troop of cavalry at his command, would it make any difference in this fight?

He grabbed Lottie's traces, murmuring, "Come on, girl. I'm taking you home." The sisters were all ready, each one with a long staff to give them strength for the road to Pharaoh.

And so off they went, to reclaim their father's treasure.

56

The first miles were quiet. They passed no one on the road till they saw the white steeple of the Pharaoh Methodist Church poking up above the trees.

That close to town, a few folks were out. A wagon rattled by, with two boys on the driver's bench. In the back was a block of carved marble. Roddy turned to watch the wagon go past. "A gravestone," he said. "They're taking that stone out to the cemetery."

The older boy in the wagon turned, as though he felt Roddy's eyes. He nodded a greeting. It was strange to see such a thing, two strangers carting a gravestone around. It was oddly comforting too. "Ashes to ashes and dust to dust," Roddy said under his breath.

Thea asked him what he'd said.

"That's what the preacherman says at a funeral. Ashes to

ashes." The wagon went around a bend in the road and was gone. "And dust to dust."

Now they were in town, going straight down the street to Mr. Queed's ropeworks. They don't look like princesses, Roddy thought. Just three ordinary girls come to get what was rightfully theirs.

They went by the church, and the Endwell Tavern. The door on the tavern came open as they passed and two men stood staring. "They must never have seen a mule before," Roddy said. But none of the girls laughed, or even smiled, at his joke.

More people were gathered, watching the procession as it headed toward Mr. Queed's. In front of the general store, a gaggle of little children were pointing and making comments. The metallic clang at the blacksmith shop ceased as they went by. A man with no shirt, but wearing a heavy leather apron, came out to see.

A shutter slammed open on a second-story window. And a girl looked down from above. It was clear what had happened since Roddy had left Pharaoh. Mr. Queed had been telling outright vicious lies about King Ivars and the girls. Now everyone in town thought of them as monsters, or at least as strange foreigners who must not be welcomed there.

A toothless old man waved his cane and croaked out the words, "Go on back. Go away." But they didn't turn around. "Witches! Witches!" the old man cried.

Two mothers swept their little children up in their arms and hurried away toward their homes.

Then Roddy saw someone he knew. Uriah Nottworth was standing at the edge of the crowd. However, getting just one glimpse of Roddy and the sisters, he sprinted away, toward the ropeworks.

In a few minutes they were there, waiting before the great gray building. Mr. Queed's house stood beyond, but it looked empty. "They're still working," Roddy said. Then he listened, and faintly there came to his ears a low groaning sound. The crank, he thought. Someone new is turning the crank.

Behind them, the crowd was quiet as an army awaiting the order to charge. Shoe leather creaked. Somebody coughed. Flies were buzzing and a little boy slapped at his neck. But the quiet was deep enough that Roddy could hear now other sounds from inside the ropeworks.

A low hum, the lines stretched tight and twisting, came to his ears.

"I'll take Lottie back to the stable," he said.

Nyxie grabbed at his sleeve, saying, "No, no," but Thea brushed her hand aside.

In the few minutes it took to get Lottie back in her stall, something had changed.

The sound from inside the ropeworks was gone. The boys had put down their hemp combs. They'd let go the crank. And Mr. Queed had ceased his endless marching back and forth.

"Go back where you came from," somebody murmured in the crowd. An apple core was thrown, almost hitting Thea in the face.

"Witches!" a mother kept saying, louder and louder.

"Shall you suffer a witch to live?" another woman said, echoing something she'd heard in church.

A rock was thrown, then a few sticks. "Princess witch!" a boy shouted.

"No! You shall not suffer a witch to live!"

Then the great double doors on the ropeworks swung open.

Roddy had only been away for a week. But in that time, something had changed. The ropeworks now seemed like a vast cave where something evil lived. He'd worked there for months. And the whole time he'd accepted it as perfectly normal. Now, the lines and pulleys, the creaking shadows, seemed too awful to face.

Thea came up beside him and slid her hand into his. "We can go back," she whispered. "If you think we cannot —"

"No," Roddy said. "We came to get your silver back. We've got to finish what we started."

Frank Beasling was waiting there by the doors. He was sneering as usual. Still, he didn't seem so sure of himself. "You come back for your job? Tired of playing games with your girlfriends?"

"Where is Mr. Queed?" Roddy asked.

Now Charlie and Lester had come out, squinting in the low sunset light. And Uriah too was there, staring at these strange visitors.

"You've got to give that silver back," Roddy said. "It belongs to King Ivars."

"There are no kings in America," a voice said from inside the ropeworks. "No such thing. We have democracy here." Mr. Queed appeared. The boys fell away to let him pass. He'd bought himself a new suit of clothes, with a hat and shiny black boots. He was puffed up bigger than ever, like a rooster proud of his plumes.

"We don't allow kings here. No man should be born to riches and power. You have to work here. Idle hands are the Devil's workshop." He was talking like a preacher, loud and sure of himself. "But busy hands are —"

"You stole the silver," Roddy said. "And we came to take it back."

"Where's your king?" Mr. Queed said, sneering. "Where's his royal army to enforce his will? I just see three girls and a weakling boy who should never have gone off from his job. Now there's no work for him. I got a new boy to turn the crank." Only then did Roddy see a face he didn't recognize. It peeped out from the shadows, with hair so blond it was almost white. The new boy looked small and young and scared.

"Just give us enough to live on," Thea said. "You can have the rest."

"No," Mr. Queed said, smiling. "I can have it all."

Frank Beasling had gone back into the building. Now he reappeared, dragging a long, brand-new rope.

"Witches!" somebody shouted. The crowd was edging

nearer to Roddy and the girls. "Witches are for hanging!"

Mr. Queed took hold of the rope's end. He looped it around and started tying a knot. Soon he had a hangman's noose.

"You hear what the good people of Pharaoh say." Mr. Queed dangled the noose.

Some of the crowd were murmuring and whispering, "Yes, yes."

"This is a democracy here. What the people want, the people shall have," Mr. Queed announced.

Roddy began to back away. But Thea held tight to his hand, anchoring him to the spot. "We are strangers in your land. That is true," she said, trying to keep the quiver out of her voice. "We do not understand how things are here. We will keep on going. We will pack up today and leave this place. Just give us back what is rightfully ours."

Mr. Queed held the noose high over his head.

"I've told the good people of Pharaoh how your father trafficked with spirits. How he conjured up the crows. How he cast spells to find treasure."

"That's not true!" Roddy shouted. "He's a peaceful old man. He just likes to read about —"

"Exactly!" Mr. Queed replied. "Tell the good townspeople

what kind of books King Ivars brought with him from the old country. Books of magic, books of spells and conjuring. Are they in English? No! They are written in strange old tongues that only a wizard, or his three witch-girls, can understand."

He came closer, still bearing the noose. "Go on, princess. Talk for the people here. Nice and loud! Let them hear what kind of tongue you speak."

Over the noise of the crowd, over Mr. Queed's taunting and Frank Beasling's murmurs of "that's right, that's right," Roddy heard a crow cawing.

It was far-off at first, a lonesome raggedy shout. But as Mr. Queed preached on, about bad foreigners and evil magic, the crow came nearer.

"We will go," Thea begged. "We will go away this night. Just give us something to pay our way."

"I'll give you something!" Mr. Queed cried and thrust the noose in Thea's face.

Now the crow had appeared, perched on the steeple of the church. It screamed one long blast of black noise, and all the hubbub ceased below.

Everyone looked up. Mr. Queed let the noose hang limp. The rope-monkeys edged out of the building to get a better look. Roddy turned, and the girls too, watching the great black bird.

It squawked again, ruffled its feathers, then was still.

By then the sun was almost down, casting long shadows across the street and among the buildings of Pharaoh. The silence stretched, like the lines in the ropeworks, stretched until it was ready to snap.

57

Was it him? Thea wondered, as she stared up at the crow. Had he come from his Court of Shadows deep in the Bastery Wood? Was he there to stake his claim on her a final time?

She eased her hand out from Roddy's grasp and walked toward the church. The crow stirred, flapped his wings a few times, but did not take flight yet.

He watched her, as the cleverest of birds watches a farmer come with a rifle. He knew the safe distance. He knew when he must flee.

Thea stopped. Now the light from the setting sun was only hitting the upper reaches, the treetops and peak of the church steeple.

Yes, it was him, she thought. His eyes shone like two gold coins. Scalander had come to be near her one last time.

"See!" Mr. Queed shouted, pointing at the bird. "See, she traffics with creatures of the night. At her beck and call, such birds of ill omen appear!"

Thea ignored his ranting. And the people too were not listening to him anymore. They all stared upward, as though waiting for the crow to speak some terrible message.

Below was deepening shadow. Above, the last red rays of sunset. The bird perched still as a weathercock on a windless day.

Mr. Queed started up again, but someone threw an apple core and hit him in the chest. "Shut him up!" a man shouted.

Then there was silence, long and broad.

Thea wasn't afraid. And she didn't know why. At any minute the crowd might turn on her again, shouting and waving their fists. Or Mr. Queed might lunge at her and snap the noose around her neck. Worse, far worse, she knew who it was perched on the steeple, and knew what rage might still burn in his heart after what she'd done to him the night before.

All the same, she wasn't afraid.

She wondered what he could see from his steeple-top vantage point. Like a king in his highest castle tower, Scalander could survey the land for miles around him. And as night fell, it was more truly his again. He was again the dark king, ruler of the dark realm.

And still, Thea was unafraid.

Mr. Queed began again, trying to get the crowd fired up

with anger. He'd only said a few words when another voice made him cease.

"Go on! Go on back home!" It was Fecula, shouting in a voice like a spitting, hissing torch. "All of you go away. This is none of your business now."

She tottered toward them, poking ahead of herself with her cane. In just one day, it seemed she'd grown twice as old. Her back was bent, and her head bobbed as she went. Her pace was slow, as though every step caused her deep pain.

"Go! All of you." As she neared the crowd, people started to edge away. She raised her cane and waved it at them. And they backed quickly down the side alleys and into buildings. "Go! This is between us and the pretty ones. If you know what's good for you, you'll get moving now and not turn around till you're home."

A little boy lingered, staring at the strange old woman. But his mother quickly snatched him up and hurried off.

"All of you! Every one!"

Soon the street was empty but for Mr. Queed, and Roddy and the girls. Even Frank Beasling and the other boys had fled into the safety of the ropeworks.

"Give me that!" Fecula croaked at Mr. Queed.

Before he could act, she grabbed the noose from him. "What do you mean by this foolishness?"

"They came for their silver. They said they wanted—"

"So give it to them!" she screamed. "Give them their silver, and let's be done with this forever. No bride for my darling. No silver for you," Fecula said.

"It's mine!" Mr. Queed sounded like a little boy, wheedling his mother for a piece of candy.

With a quick snap of her arm, Fecula got the noose around his neck and pulled it up tight. "Your little rope-monkey ruined it all. He led the old king out to the woods. He came between my darling boy and his intended bride. You sold him for a handful of coins, and he ruined everything. If you'd have kept him here at the crank, working as he ought to, then you'd have all your silver right now. And my darling would have his queen."

The crow let loose with one wild cry, as if to shout his agreement.

"None of us, not you nor me nor my darling boy, can have what we desire."

"But there she is," Mr. Queed croaked. "Take her. She's yours. Nobody can stop you. Take her for your boy."

"It's too late for that," Mother Fecula said. "Last night, at midnight, was the moment. And now it's gone." She came at Thea, pulling Mr. Queed along by the noose around his neck.

"This one," she growled, pointing her cane at Thea, "this one hurt my boy. She hurt him bad with her flaming torch. And now look at him. Look!" She jerked the noose upward. Mr. Queed and all the others turned their eyes skyward. The dusklight was completely gone now. Scalander was just a blur, a smudge of blackness at the tip of the steeple.

"Look at him!" she commanded. "Fire and spite hurt my boy. A fiery torch and a girl's cruel spite."

"That is not true," Thea said. "It was no spite. I just did the right thing. You cannot make a girl . . ." She paused, trying to find the words. Her voice got louder. "It was wrong, and you know it."

"Don't talk to me about right and wrong!" Fecula growled. "You stabbed my darling in his heart. You put fire to him. You burned him back to that!" She pointed at the steeple.

Thea heard the flap of wings. The high shadows moved, like clouds driven by a night wind. And Scalander was gone.

58

"It's over. It's all over," Fecula said, pulling Mr. Queed close. "Now tell your boys to gather up the silver and give it back."

He started to argue. But she yanked the noose tight and hissed at him. "Do it now. Or I'll string you from the steeple top. I swear it. I will."

So Mr. Queed gave the order to his rope-monkeys, and soon enough they were rolling two casks of silver out into the street.

Roddy went to the stable and hitched up a wagon. He drove it around to where the boys stood, and helped them roll the barrels up two sagging planks.

From where he sat, on the wagon's high bench, he could see into the ropeworks. A few lanterns burned there, making the lines look like a great spider's web. And there was his crank, where he'd worked so hard for so long. This was the last time he'd see it. He was certain of that. No matter what happened now. He'd never come back to this place.

The other boys cowered in the ropeworks, afraid to be seen, but afraid also of missing anything that happened.

Nyxie and Mina climbed into the back of the wagon. Thea joined Roddy on the bench. He turned the mules and headed back toward the Seven house.

The whole way home no one said a word. All three of the girls, and Roddy too, kept their eyes to the sky, looking for a sign that Scalander was following.

But they saw nothing, and heard no sound of wings.

5 9

King Ivars was still asleep when they returned. The girls all
filed into his room and circled around the bed. Mina held a
candle. Nyxie whispered, "Shouldn't we tell him?"

"Let him sleep," Thea said. "He was so weak. He can see
the silver in the morning."

Roddy stood in the doorway. He wanted to join the girls
around the bed. But no matter what he'd gone through with
them, still King Ivars was their father, not his.

He hung back, trying to get a peek at the old king without
intruding. They seemed so happy then. All the sisterly squabbles
were over, all their worries about the silver at an end.

"Thea," Ivars murmured.

"We're right here, Papa." She leaned in and took his hand.
"We're back and everything's going to be fine now. We got the
silver back."

The king nodded weakly, as though Thea had said, "We brought you a cup of tea."

"You go back to sleep now, and we'll tell you all about it in the morning."

"Good girls," he said. "You're all good girls."

Roddy waited for some mention of him. He wanted to hear Ivars say his name as he did his daughters'. But the king fell back into sleep, and Thea ushered them all out of the room.

"Nyxie, you need to be in bed too." For once, Nyxie did as she was told without complaining.

Roddy knelt before the fire and blew on the coals. He placed a few shreds of pine tinder on the coals and got a little flicker of flame. Then he added kindling and soon they had a fire.

"Are you going to bed?" Thea asked.

"I guess I'll sit up for a while. I've got a lot of thinking to do." Roddy was afraid if he closed his eyes and went to sleep, it all would come back, even more real than before. The forest journey, the terrible black creature, the old woman's curses and threats. And then what he'd seen just a few hours before.

Thea sat down nearby. "I suppose you can go back to your mother and father now."

Roddy shrugged. "They'll be angry to see me. I didn't serve out my time with Mr. Queed."

"After all that happened? If you tell them how bad it all was, what you have gone through, they will surely be glad to take you back."

"Maybe. And maybe not." He poked at the fire with a stick. A cloud of sparks swirled up like a swarm of glowing bugs. "They made a bargain with Mr. Queed."

"I am so tired of hearing about bargains!" Thea said. "You are not . . . we are not pigs and sheep to be traded away."

"I suppose."

Thea got up and looked for something to eat. There was a pan of corn bread half gone. The edges were all burned. Mina still had a lot to learn about cooking. But when Thea held it out, Roddy scooped out a big handful and ate without complaint.

She had what was left, washing it down with cider from a clay jug.

"So what will you do?" Roddy asked after a while. "You can't stay here anymore."

"No, we will have to move on," Thea said. "When Papa is

strong enough, we can get a wagon and a mule and head out west, I suppose. There is plenty of land that way, no? Perhaps we can find a place where there will not be any people who hate us for who we are."

The fire crackled and hissed. Roddy felt exhaustion like bags of sand pressing on every part of his body. He wanted to sleep, badly. But every time he closed his eyes, he saw Fecula sneering and snapping at him. He saw the noose and the look of pure motherly rage on her face.

"You can start again in a better place," Roddy said. "You've got the silver. You can buy a thousand acres somewhere and hire folks to work it. Soon enough you'll be living like you did in the old country. You'll have rich boys coming to see you. A big house where you can have dances and parties and fine music all night. Soon enough this will all be nothing. You'll hardly remember it. And me too."

"That is not true," she said, taking his hand in both of hers. "How could we forget you? Not after all the help—"

"Help!" he exclaimed, before she could finish. "There you go. I'm the helper. The servant boy. I was good at turning the crank. I always do as I'm told. I'm good at working around the farm. But you'll find somebody else to do that. You've got the silver to hire a dozen more boys to help out."

"Why are you talking this way?" Thea said. Her eyes were getting shiny with tears. "Why are you so angry?"

"It's simple as pie. Because I got nowhere to go. My family doesn't want to see me till my seven years are up. And I'm not going back to the ropeworks. So where does that leave me?"

She squeezed his hand. "Come with us."

"Where?"

"Wherever we go. West, or south. Or Canada. Papa said it is only a hundred miles away. Does it matter? Just someplace far from here, far from these people."

Roddy didn't talk for a long time. The logs and sticks settled on the hearth. The flames all dwindled to glowing coals.

Roddy liked it that Thea was near. He liked the feel of her hands. And even the look of tears in her eyes. This was all nice. A friend and a fire. And soon sleep. But what about tomorrow?

He got up finally, saying, "I can't keep my eyes open anymore."

She nodded and said good night, first in German, like a little mother. Then in English as his friend.

60

The two casks of silver were standing by the door when Thea went out the next morning to get water. But the wagon was gone. "Where's Roddy?" Mina asked, as they were eating breakfast. "Doesn't he want any?"

"He must have taken the wagon back to town."

They heard stirrings in their father's room and went to see. King Ivars was up, sitting on the edge of the bed. His arms and legs looked thin as old twine. And his hair stood out like a thundercloud. But the fogginess was gone from his eyes. When he spoke, Thea knew he was fully himself again.

"A beautiful morning," he said. His door was open, and the main house door too. So he could look straight outside. "Nice warm sunshine. A good sign."

The girls all came in and helped him to stand. He went unsteadily to the kitchen with them. But with each step, it seemed he gained some of his strength.

"Where is Roddy?" he asked. Mina got to work, heating water for his coffee. Thea slid a plate of corn bread over to her father. He broke off a piece and nibbled. "Where is the boy? It will take both of us to get the silver back today."

The girls explained what had happened the day before. Each one chimed in, butted in, eager to tell the story. By the time they'd gotten it all said, Ivars was outside, looking at the two casks. He pried back the top on one. And yes, it was all there, glinting in the morning sun.

He sat down on the other, pouring a bright spill from hand to hand. "He did this? Roddy got it back from them?"

"No," Nyxie said. "Not just him. We all did. Well, mostly Thea and Roddy. But we were all there."

"He's a good boy. A very good boy," Ivars murmured. Then louder: "So where is he? I owe him my thanks."

"Thea said he took the wagon back to town."

"I'm not sure. I just thought he must have. Where else would he go?"

King Ivars stood, and with no help, went back into the house. With each step he took, he got stronger.

*6**1***

Roddy took the wagon to the edge of town. There he saw a father and son walking back from the river. Each had a few fish on a string, their breakfast, most likely.

"Can you drive this wagon back to the ropeworks?" Roddy asked. "Are you going that way?"

The man said he would. "It'll take a little load off my feet." Roddy got down and the two climbed up.

"You know where it is?" Roddy asked. "Mr. Queed's ropeworks?"

"Of course. Who doesn't know? Everybody's been talking about —"

"That's right," Roddy said. "That's the place."

He thanked the man and watched him drive away. The father and son, he noticed, looked like two versions of the same person. The same shock of blond hair, the same broad mouth and flattish nose. The man might have been the boy, twenty years before.

As the wagon disappeared, Roddy thought of his own father. Never once had he gone fishing with him. Never had they done anything just the two of them. How could he with nine children? It wasn't possible. Still, the sight of the two with their strings of fish, stabbed a hot pang into Roddy's heart.

"I can't go back," he said aloud. "They don't want me." A blue jay was screaming in the nearby brush, as though arguing with Roddy. "If they wanted me, they wouldn't have sent me away."

The bird flew up suddenly, a rush of brilliant blue. It squawked again, and perched in a birch tree. He thought of his mother, always complaining, scolding, saying he was wrong, wrong, wrong.

He headed back the way he'd come. But shortly, he heard the jay screaming again. He saw a side trail and without knowing where it led, set off that way.

More sure than ever that he couldn't return to his family, he thought now about King Ivars and the girls. Did they really want him? Or was it just pity he heard in Thea's voice last night? She'd said, "Come with us." It sounded sincere. He knew she wouldn't lie to him. But for her to feel sorry for him, that he couldn't stand. He'd rather be back at the ropeworks crank, or even plowing the fields with the slaver's whip cracking over his head, than be treated with pity.

He wandered across a meadow. There, the buzz of locusts seemed to fill the whole world. It was loud as God's grindstone, when he sharpens the great sword of wrath. Loud and unending. Loud and hard as steel. And like the noise of the ropeworks, it drove away all other sounds, all other thoughts.

Roddy stood awhile in the hot morning sun, all by himself. He stood and let the locusts' buzz fill him up. No mother and father. No home.

The noise rose as if the grindstone were spinning faster. No work at the crank. No old king and pretty daughters.

The noise swelled as though the metal edge were being forced against the spark-spitting stone. No Thea, saying he should come with them. No Thea to hold his hand and say she wanted him along. No Thea, beautiful and proud and brave in the face of terrible danger.

Suddenly, Roddy couldn't stand the locusts' noise anymore.

He shouted at the top of his voice. Not a word, but a raw burst of rage. He shouted, and then there was silence. The locusts' seething din died. And silence flooded the meadow.

He readied to make the noise again, to shout back at the locusts. But they stayed still as long as he stood there.

62

They wasted no time preparing to leave Pharaoh. That very day, the girls began packing up their things. Blankets and bedding. The skillet, which Mina scoured with sand. Some plates and cups. Rope and needles, scissors, and of course all of King Ivars's books.

Without Roddy, they couldn't get the silver casks inside. Even with all of them huffing and straining, the casks barely moved. So King Ivars decided to divide the treasure up among smaller containers.

By dinnertime they had a few leather sacks filled with silver, and two pitchers from the springhouse. A wooden cigar box was full, as were a butter tub, the pockets of an apron, an oaken bucket, and Nyxie's tiny purse.

"I'll go into town tomorrow. As soon as the sun rises," Ivars said. "I'll buy the first wagon and team that I see. And before the sun is straight up, we'll have put a good number of miles behind us."

Thea asked, "Isn't Roddy coming with us?"

"If he wants," King Ivars said. "Not if he doesn't. Where's he gotten off to, anyway?"

"I don't know," she whispered. The dread of losing Roddy gnawed at her.

When they'd done all the packing they could, Thea went to look for him. Down the road to town, but not too far. Around the nearby fields. And even along the path to the Bastery Wood. The great green wall loomed up as she approached. He would never go back there, she thought. Not after what he'd seen there. Still, she followed the trail almost to the edge of the woods.

Should she call out his name?

No. She carried her own silence like a heavy pack on her back. If Roddy had gone that way, then he didn't want to be found. No point in yelling and blubbering. Still, Thea stood a long while looking into the leafy shadowy depths.

When Thea got back home, Mina was just finishing up their evening meal. Nyxie was setting the table, singing under her breath. And her father was outside with a hatchet, splitting up kindling for the morning fire.

He looked healthier than he had in months. The fever had taken him close to death. But she wondered if it had been good for him, burning away the old sickness and exhaustion. His arm cocked back and came down again and again. Each time, he let out a little grunt, and smiled to see the pinewood pop into two clean halves.

The pile was already bigger than they'd need.

"I didn't see him," Thea said. "And I looked everywhere."

"Perhaps he returned to his family. Where was it? Rector's Ford?"

"No. He'd never go back there." She sat down on a stump and watched her father balance another stick to be split. "He's got no place in the world. We don't have a home. We lost the castle and the land and our true place. But at least we've got each other. He's got nowhere and nobody."

"We can leave a note on the door here saying which way we went."

"What if he never returns here?"

"Then I suppose he'll ask along the way if he wants to find us. How many other old men and three daughters will be traveling along with a wagon full of books and good German silver?"

"But what if he doesn't follow us?"

"Then he wants to be somewhere else."

Mina came out and said it was time to eat. And with that, they talked no more about it.

63

Roddy spent the night under the stars. There was no moon, no clouds to speak of, no wind. He lay in a meadow perhaps a mile from the old Seven place, and stared up at the sky.

He thought of King Ivars's Ten Thousand Charms and wondered if there were stars enough that night to assign one to every charm. He tried counting them but didn't know enough numbers.

The locusts were silent now. There'd been an owl in a nearby tree, but he'd swooped off in search of prey and not come back. A dog was barking, far far away. But even he ceased after a while, as though the vastness of the sky had swallowed up his noise.

This silence had a different quality than in daytime. It wasn't the absence of sound exactly. No, it was the presence of something else. Something that pushed all the pain and loss and loneliness away. He supposed Preacher Dow would have called it "the spirit of the Holy One," or something like that. Roddy didn't know about such things. He had no fancy words as folks used when talking of religion. But he did know that something vast and good was watching over him.

If he could just stay here forever, he'd be happy. If the sun didn't rise and the birds didn't wake singing. If the wind stayed away, and the voices of people didn't reach him there, then he'd never move from this spot.

The Milky Way stretched over his head, an endless arch of white silence. It stood guard as he fell asleep, and remained there till the rising sun burned it away.

•

64

King Ivars was back before noon the next day with a wagon and a great, one-eyed ox to pull it. "The blacksmith, that robber, he charged me twice what he's worth," Ivars said, slapping the huge beast on the flank. "But I don't mind. I like this ox just fine."

They got to work piling their belongings into the wagon.

"Where are we going?" Nyxie kept asking as they packed.

"West," her father said.

"Ohio? Indiana? Wisconsin?" Nyxie had been studying her geography and thought herself quite an expert.

"Just west," Ivars said. "Till we find the place that's right for us."

With a last wander through the house, he declared that they were ready to leave.

Thea was writing a note for Roddy, in case he came back.

> *Papa says we will go due west. We have a red ox now*
> *to pull the wagon. So just ask along the way about him*

because he only has one eye and when it rains his coat
gets the color of blood. Maybe he's our last charm here.

You have to come and join us wherever we go. You're
better than welcome to be with us. You know that. So
just go west from here and you will find us soon enough.

Your true friend,

Thea

She nailed the note on the front door, good and secure. Then she joined the rest of them at the wagon.

"What if he doesn't find it?" Nyxie said. "What if it gets blown away or somebody comes and takes it down?"

"He'll find us," King Ivars said, and gave the ox a swat to get him moving.

After going only a few miles, they saw someone waiting. The road rose there, up a hill, and the figure was standing in silhouette. It's him, Thea thought. There he is waiting for us. She sat up taller, straining her eyes.

The other girls saw him too and waved. But he didn't wave back.

"Papa," Thea said. "There he is."

"I'm not so sure," her father said.

"It must be him."

But as they drew closer, dismay filled Thea like cold rain pouring into a cistern. It wasn't Roddy, but a man. He had a peddler's pack on his back, and leaned on a walking staff.

He wanted a ride on the wagon. King Ivars said he was sorry, but they had no room. Indeed, going up hills, the girls all had to get off to make it easier on the ox. As it was, they had to nestle into spots between the tools and the bedding and the crates of books.

"You have likely seen a boy?" King Ivars asked in clumsy English.

Thea asked with a smoother tongue.

"No. Just me and Mr. Stick." The man struck his walking staff on the dusty road. "You sure you can't spare a little space?"

King Ivars shook his head. "We are sorry," Thea said. "We are overloaded as it is."

And so they went on, over the hillrise. Just at the top, they got a view of this new place. The river snaked and coiled the whole length of the broad Genesee valley. Thea had never had such a view, miles and miles in every direction. The green of woodlands, and the brighter green of corn and wheat ripening in strong sunshine.

"There," Ivars said, pointing far away. "Way down there. A bridge. We'll cross the river there."

65

Roddy went back toward the old Seven house. But getting a glimpse of it, the cold, empty feeling welled up in him again. That wasn't his home, he told himself again. He had no place there. He had no place anywhere.

So he stood a ways off, watching, hoping to get one more glimpse of the girls. Of Thea especially.

No one appeared. No voices or sounds of life came from the house.

"They're gone," he said aloud, after a while. "They're gone, and I'm still here."

He approached the house from the side, like a spy sneaking up on an enemy fort. He crept to one window, listened, then peered in. "Gone," he said. The house was empty. Nothing of the girls or Ivars remained. Even the ashes had been swept out of the hearth.

He wanted to shout out his pain, but he wasn't much for

cursing. He wanted to break the window, every window there. Tear the door off. Smash holes in the walls with his fists.

Instead, he sucked down a few long deep breaths, and turned away.

By the well, he saw a curve of rust-red metal in the weeds. It was the crown he and Ivars had found. He picked it up and turned it slowly. He was about to toss it down the well, sneering "Hail to Prince Roddy," when he heard a far-off sound.

Just the wind, he told himself. But it kept on, like a faint voice.

He listened harder, and, yes, there were words in the distant sigh of the wind. Or just one word: "west."

He placed the iron crown on his head, no longer sneering. Indeed Ivars had called him Prince Roddy when he crowned him that day. It was foolishness, the softheaded whim of a softheaded old man. Still, Roddy left the crown on his head. It's just the rusted rim of an old bucket. That's what he told himself. But he left it there. And he thought of Ivars saying for the girls to hear, "Prince Roddy."

The wind kept up its lonely moan. Roddy turned to the west and set off in that direction.

After a few hours he came to the crest of a ridge. There, below him, the valley of the Genesee spread out green and wide and serene. A road cut through the fields, going west. In places it disappeared, where the woods were thick or the corn grew high. But it was clear most of the way to the bridge.

Roddy stood a long time, watching a tiny black blur move along the road. A wagon, he supposed, pulled by a mule. No, it was too big for a mule. Perhaps a great dray horse, or an ox.

Three figures were walking alongside the wagon.

"West." The far-off voice came on the breath of the wind.

"West," Prince Roddy said. And he set off toward the river.